This book is lovingly dedicated to my father, Clarence Stroda. Rest in peace, Dad.

Beloved, think it not strange concerning the fiery trial which is to try you, as though some strange thing happened unto you: But rejoice, inasmuch as ye are partakers of Christ's sufferings; that, when his glory shall be revealed, ye may be glad also with exceeding joy.

—*1 Peter* 4:12–13

Chapter One

Inside Philadelphia's noisy bus terminal, Mari Kemp clasped both hands to her chest, overjoyed at this unexpected turn of events in her desperate adventure. "You're going to Fort Craig, Maine, too? This is *wunderbar*. Have you been there before? What's it like? Do you have family there?"

She leaned forward eager for any information about the place and her traveling companion.

An *Englisch* friend had driven Mari from her home in the Amish community of Arthur, Illinois, to Champagne to catch a bus during the wee hours of the morning. Mary Kate Brenneman got on in Columbus, Ohio. Mari didn't realize they shared the same destination until they were changing buses during a layover in Philadelphia. Now, waiting for their boarding call in the busy terminal, Mari couldn't have been happier. Mary

Kate wasn't exactly the talkative, friendly type, but that didn't deter Mari.

"Tell me everything you can about Fort Craig."

"I haven't been there," Mary Kate said. "I have only exchanged letters with a young man who lives in the area."

"An Amish fellow? What's his name? What does he say it is like?"

"His name is Asher Fisher. He wrote about his family farm. Potatoes are the main crop in the area. There are many large farms."

Mari struggled to hide her disappointment. "I thought there would be lots of wild forests to explore."

Cornfields surrounded her home in Arthur. Nothing for miles and miles except corn and more corn. Potato fields would be different, at least.

"Mr. Fisher did not mention forests," Mary Kate said.

Mari waited for more information, but Mary Kate wasn't forthcoming. Mari forged ahead. "I'm going to visit my grandmother. Perhaps Mr. Fisher has mentioned Naomi Helmuth. They might belong to the same church district." Did her grandmother still practice the Amish faith?

"There is only one Amish congregation near Fort Craig at a place called New Covenant. I don't recall him mentioning the name Helmuth.

I'm getting off the bus near the settlement. It's about three miles from Fort Craig."

It was too much to hope for information about the grandmother Mari had never met. She would simply stick to the plan. She hadn't written to say she was coming. A letter could be returned unopened, as they had all been in the past, but a long-lost granddaughter standing on Naomi Helmuth's doorstep couldn't be ignored. At least that was Mari's hope.

It had shocked her to learn that her father had been estranged from his mother since before Mari was born. Mari had assumed her grandparents had both passed away. When her father died recently, she discovered letters he had written to his mother over the years all returned unopened. The last one had been addressed to her in Fort Craig, Maine, a year ago. That was where Mari intended to start her search. She hadn't heard of New Covenant until now.

Her father had been a kind and loving man, raising Mari alone after her mother died when she was barely four. She had been incredibly close to her father. Only God had been more important than family to Raymond Kemp. Finding out his mother was alive, a fact he'd never mentioned, was unfathomable to Mari. Something terrible must have happened for him to keep such a secret from her. She wouldn't rest until she learned what had driven a wedge between mother and son and why he hid the truth. The hope of a joyful reception with her grandmother was slim, but Naomi Helmuth was the only family Mari had left in the world. She was the one person who had answers. Mari wouldn't leave Maine without them. Her father used to say she was stubborn to a fault. She could be when something was important.

"Mary Kate? Is that you?"

"Sarah?" Mary Kate's voice trembled with disbelief as she surged to her feet.

"*Gott* be praised, it is you." A woman squealed with delight and threw her arms around Mary Kate. She wore a modest blue print dress with a small black prayer covering pinned to her hair. Mari assumed she was Old Order Mennonite, not Amish.

"Sarah, dear, dear, Sarah." The two women clung to each other, overcome with emotion. After several long moments, Mary Kate recovered her composure and sat down beside Mari again, still holding on to Sarah's hand. "What are you doing here?"

Sarah sank to her knees in front of Mary Kate. "My husband and I are returning from his uncle's funeral. What are you doing here?"

Mary Kate gave a nervous laugh. "I'm on my way to Maine."

"Maine? Whatever for? Don't tell me Edmond is taking you on vacation."

Looking down, Mary Kate shook her head. "Edmond passed away two years ago."

"Dearest, cousin. I'm so sorry."

"*Gott* allowed it," Mary Kate whispered.

"We cannot comprehend His ways," Sarah said.

Mary Kate looked up. "We can't, but He has brought you and I together again. Oh, you don't know how glad I am to see you. It's been what? Ten years."

"Eleven. I can't believe I've run into you here, of all places. You must come meet my children. I have a son and two daughters. They've gone out to the van that is taking us back to Bird-in-Hand. I stopped to get something to drink for on the way. If I hadn't, I would have missed seeing you. *Gott ist goot*. Who is this with you?"

Mari held out her hand. "A complete stranger who happens to be going to Maine on the same bus. I'm Mari Kemp." She prayed her meeting with her grandmother was half as joy filled as the reunion of these two women.

"I'm pleased to meet you. My wits are scattered to the wind. Oh, Mary Kate, we should never have lost touch. I should have tried harder. We were closer than sisters once."

"It wasn't your fault. Edmond forbade it, and he was set in his ways."

"It's not right to speak ill of him, but he caused us both so much pain. I wasn't baptized into the Amish faith when I jumped the fence to marry. Edmond should have allowed us to remain friends. Tell me, why are you going to Maine of all places?"

"To get married."

"You have met someone new and fallen in love. Oh, Mary Kate, I'm so happy for you." Sarah hugged her again.

Mary Kate pulled away from her cousin. "Not exactly. Mr. Fisher and I haven't actually met."

Mari frowned. "I thought you said you were getting married."

"That is my plan. We've been corresponding."

"I don't understand," Sarah said. "You're planning to marry someone you haven't met?"

"I am."

Sarah looked stunned. "Why?"

Mary Kate gripped her hands together. "Things have become too difficult to remain at home. I couldn't stay there any longer. I took a chance and answered an ad placed by a bishop looking for Amish individuals willing to join a new community in northern Maine. He put me in touch with Asher Fisher, a very kind man. We, how do I say it, we connected in our letters. This is my only chance of getting my son back, Sarah."

"What on earth do you mean?"

"I'm ashamed to say after Ed died, I fell to pieces. I could barely function. Our son was only three. Ed's sister and her husband took him in until I could get back on my feet. I saw him often, but the business was in trouble, and it took so much of my time. Ed dreamed our son would run it one day. I thought I needed to save it, but the cost was too high. I was horribly unhappy. I missed Matthew, but I truly thought for a time that he was better off with Ed's sister. To make a long story short, I eventually sold the business. There was a terrible family row over it, and my in-laws refused to relinquish my son. They said the boy needed a father."

"How unfair to you and your child," Sarah declared. "Surely your bishop intervened?"

"He agreed with them. But he said if I married again that would change things."

Sarah clasped Mary Kate's hands. "You poor dear, but is marrying a stranger halfway across the country the answer? Isn't there a man in your community you could turn to?"

Mary Kate looked away. "That wasn't possible."

Mari's heart ached for the young mother. How awful to be kept from her child.

Sighing deeply, Mary Kate gazed at her cousin. "Now that I'm on my way, I'm not sure I'm doing the right thing. Even if it's for the right reason."

The PA system came on to announce Mari's bus was boarding now. She picked up her suitcase. "That's us."

Sarah gripped Mary Kate's hand. "I can't be parted from you so soon."

"We'll write. Give me your address."

"*Nee.* You must come and stay with me. You need time to consider this decision. Mr. Fisher can wait a week or two. I'll buy you another ticket to Maine when you're tired of my company. Please, dear cousin, say you'll stay with me for a little while. I'll help you sort this out."

Mary Kate's eyes filled with tears. "I wish I could, but Asher is meeting this bus."

Mari wanted to help. "I'm going to the same destination. I can deliver a message to Mr. Fisher in person and explain you've been delayed by family matters."

Hope filled Mary Kate's eyes, then quickly faded. "I can't do that to Asher. It wouldn't be fair to stand him up."

Sarah gripped Mary Kate's shoulders. "Mari will make him understand. *Gott* brought us together after all these years for a reason."

Mary Kate bit her lower lip. "I don't know what to do."

The final boarding call for their bus came over the PA system. Mari hooked her black purse over her shoulder and smiled at Mary Kate. "I find it is always best to do what your heart tells you."

Ash Fisher clenched and opened his icy fingers repeatedly as his three brothers inspected him from all angles, smoothed his vest across his chest and brushed imaginary lint from his shoulder. He wasn't exactly sure how he'd gotten himself into this situation.

That wasn't true. One impulsive moment and a stamp had sealed his fate.

Gabe, the oldest, took a step back. "You'll do."

Moses, the youngest Fisher brother, lifted Ash's black hat from the pegs by the door. "You're not nervous, are you?"

"Of course he is," Seth declared. "He's about to meet the woman he intends to marry for the first time. Who wouldn't be nervous?"

Ash snatched his hat from his little brother's hands. "I'm not nervous. I'm on my way to meet a woman who has been kind enough to correspond with me for the past three months and has simply agreed to visit for a few weeks."

He jammed his hat on his head. "That's it. She's coming for a visit and nothing else."

If only that were the whole truth.

Those around him smothered their chuckles.

He glanced up at his brim and turned his hat the right way around.

Gabe and Seth exchanged knowing looks as they leaned against each other. They were identical tall blond men who took after their father. Ash and Moses had inherited their mother's dark hair and eyes. Most people assumed Gabe and Seth were twins, but they were actually two parts of the Fisher triplets. Ash was the third.

"He's lying," Seth said.

Gabe nodded. "He's scared to death."

"Being the most sensible of this lot entitles me to a little more respect," Ash said between gritted teeth. His brothers laughed.

"You mean most stodgy," Gabe said. He was the jokester. Seth was the tenderhearted fellow. Moses was the baby brother who liked to mimic Gabe. That left Ash as the practical and meticulous one. Something his brothers seldom appreciated.

"He's the dull one." Seth shook his head sadly. He was normally sympathetic, but he enjoyed teasing Ash as much as the others did.

"Dull as ditchwater," Moses added, making a long face. The others laughed again.

Ash wasn't amused by his brothers' humor this a.m. He stared at the yawning front door standing open to a beautiful spring morning and took a deep breath. There was no going back now. He had to meet the bus.

Only, what if Mary Kate wasn't like he had imagined from her letters? What if they weren't compatible? She could hate Maine. Maybe she would turn around and head home as soon as he opened his mouth to speak and nothing witty came out. Talking to women made him nervous. They all seemed to want things he didn't understand. Would she be the same?

No. He chided himself for his lack of faith in her. Mary Kate was a practical woman. She would see his fine qualities, his head for business, his faith and his steady character. She wasn't expecting a love match. She believed mutual affection could grow over time. Her purpose for this trip was to get to know him.

That certainly had been his original plan. Nothing good ever came of impulsive actions. Why had he posted that last letter?

He glanced at his brothers. Because he was lonely, and he wanted what they had. This was a sensible way to accomplish that.

Seth and Gabe were married. Happily so. The evenings spent with his brothers and their new, loving wives made Ash feel like an outsider, separated from the brothers he had done everything with since the day they were born. He'd never felt that way before. He and his brothers had always been close. Now, inside his family's boisterous home, he was lonely.

At twenty-five, he was ready to start a family. He ran a finger underneath his tight collar. It was expected. An Amish fellow wasn't complete without a wife and family. He believed that. What he hated was the idea of wasting time looking for the right woman. The local maidens Moses wanted to impress didn't interest Ash. They were young and immature. They had nothing in common with him. Trying to talk to them made his words stick in his throat.

It hadn't been that way when he was writing to Mary Kate. Pouring out his thoughts on paper was easy. She understood. She wasn't happy in her current situation. Neither was he. It seemed fated that they should get together.

He squared his shoulders. This was the right thing to do. He wouldn't let a few minor worries stop him from following through with his plan.

Gabe straightened. "We should stop gabbing, or Ash is going to be late meeting the bride. Are you sure you don't want us to come with you? We can help break the ice."

"I would rather have all my teeth yanked out by a team of horses." Ash forced himself to walk out the door to the waiting black buggy he had carefully washed from top to bottom. The ebony paint and brass fittings gleamed in the early May sunshine. He stopped in his tracks when he saw Frisky harnessed to it.

The lively black mare was a showy high stepper that belonged to Moses. His little brother had only recently purchased the horse for his courting buggy, planning to impress some of the newly arrived young women in the community. Frisky tossed her head and pranced in place, eager to be off.

Furious, Ash turned to Moses. The last thing he needed was to look like a ridiculous teenager going courting. "I told you to hitch Dottie."

"She seemed a tad lame this morning." Moses hid his mouth with one hand, unable to keep a smirk off his face.

Seth pushed Ash toward the buggy door. "It will take too long to change horses. You don't want to be late. Frisky will make a fine impression. No fellow who drives a horse like her is dull."

Ash's need to be punctual warred with his desire to look respectable and dignified. Punctuality won. He didn't want to leave Mary Kate standing at the bus stop.

"Relax." Seth patted Ash's shoulder. "You'll love wedded bliss as much as we do."

"Will you men leave Ash alone and get in here? There's work to be done," Seth's wife yelled from the kitchen door.

"Coming, Pamela." Seth gave Ash a sheepish grin. "She's bossy, but she's a fine cook and a better kisser." He jogged toward the door.

Gabe stepped close to Ash. "You told Mary Kate that my Esther is deaf, right? I don't want their meeting to be awkward."

Ash shared a reassuring smile with his brother. "I did. She wrote she has been studying sign language. We'll make sure Esther feels included."

Gabe nodded. "I know you will. We look forward to meeting her. Now get going and hurry back. We have two new buggy orders to fill."

"Right." The Fisher family buggy business was expanding steadily, allowing all the sons to live and work on the farm, something that had been in doubt just a year ago.

Ash stepped into the buggy. It would take him twenty-five minutes to reach the bus stop on the other side of New Covenant. He didn't want to be late, but there was no point in being early. He picked up the lines and slapped them gently against the mare's rump. "Frisky, walk on."

Mary Kate had seemed nice in her letters, but there was no guarantee she'd like him in person. The closer he got to his destination, the more he wondered if courting a woman by mail was a sound plan.

When the village of New Covenant came into view, his palms started sweating. He rubbed them on his pant legs. This was ridiculous. He and Mary Kate had corresponded for months. He knew what to expect. She was the perfect woman for him. Sensible, practical, willing to work alongside him and his family. What more could he ask? Still, he kept Frisky to a walk, although she was eager to go faster.

On the other side of New Covenant, the county road sloped a curving half mile toward the main highway. Ash saw the flashing red lights and heard the wail of sirens as he approached the intersection. Police cars were blocking the road. An ambulance was pulling away. There must have been an accident. He stopped his buggy well back from the activity and looked for the bus. He didn't see it.

Should he go down and offer to help? He was debating when he caught sight of a State Police officer walking in his direction. The fellow stopped beside the buggy. "Morning. I'm Officer Melvin Peaks of the Maine State Police. You're one of the Amish folks that live in this area, right?"

"I am. What has happened?"

"There's been a hit-and-run accident. An Amish woman has been injured."

"Is it serious?" It had to be someone he knew. Their community had only two dozen families in total.

"I'm afraid she's badly hurt. We're trying to locate her next of kin."

"Who is she?"

The officer pushed his trooper's hat up with one finger. "She didn't have any identification on her, but she was clutching this."

Officer Peak held out an envelope. "It's addressed to Mary Kate Brenneman of Bounty, Ohio, from Asher Fisher. Do you know either of these people?"

"I'm Asher Fisher." His voice seemed to come from a long way off. He held out his hand for the envelope with his handwriting on it. "Mary Kate was coming to see me."

"Mary Kate, open your eyes. Can you hear me? Mary Kate? Squeeze my fingers if you can hear me."

She only wanted to sink back into the painless oblivion. It hurt too much to listen to the voice. Everything hurt. Even breathing.

"Open your eyes, Mary Kate." The insistent voice belonged to a woman.

Stop talking. Let me go back to sleep. Why do I hurt so much?

"I'm sorry, Mr. Fisher. Perhaps if you spoke to her, she might recognize your voice."

"She's never heard me speak." It was a man

who answered. "It's been two days. How long before she wakes up?"

"It's hard to say with an injury like this. Sit with her for a while and talk to her. Patients can sometimes hear even if they can't respond."

"What should I say?"

Nothing. Go away. A soft beeping sound penetrated the quiet she craved.

Something scraped across the floor. A chair maybe? She heard a heavy sigh.

"I'm sorry I was late, Mary Kate. The bus was early, but I could have been there sooner. I have no excuse. I wasn't there. You were hurt because of me. Please forgive me."

Thankfully, he fell silent. She sank toward the blessed darkness again.

"I'm not one for small talk. I'm sure I mentioned that in my letters. Your letters were nice. I looked forward to them. Nurse, I don't think she hears me."

"You're doing fine. Tell her about your family. She was coming to visit them, right?"

Why was that woman encouraging him? She just wanted silence and sleep.

"My parents are here waiting to meet you."

"Please go away," she croaked, not recognizing her own weak voice but feeling the strain of it.

"Nurse! She spoke."

A hand touched her forehead. "Open your eyes," the woman said again.

She forced her eyes open, but only her left one seemed to work. The light was too bright. She squeezed her eye shut and turned away from the brightness.

"Hello. Welcome back. How are you feeling?" the woman asked.

"Awful." Her throat was parched.

"I'm not surprised. You've been in an accident. You're in the hospital. I'm Mandy Brown. I'm your nurse."

"You were hit by a car. I'm Asher Fisher. I'm the fellow you were coming to meet."

She cracked her eye open and tried to focus on his face. He was a young man in his mid-twenties. He had on a white shirt with suspenders over his brawny shoulders and dark pants. His brown hair was cut short, but it curled enough that it didn't look austere on him. Dark eyes filled with concern gazed at her. There was nothing familiar about him. "I don't recognize you."

"We've only written to each other. We haven't met in person."

"It's time for your pain medication," the nurse said. "Now that you're awake, I need you to tell me your name and date of birth."

"It's…" *What was her name? Why couldn't she think of it?*

She started to tremble. "I don't know. Why can't I remember my name? What's wrong with me?" She struggled to sit up, but a sharp pain in her chest made her fall back with a moan.

"Your name is Mary Kate Brenneman," Asher said gently. "You're from Bounty, Ohio."

She tried again to focus on his face. She had to believe him. "You know me, right?"

"Mr. Fisher, you should step out," the nurse insisted. "I'm going to get the doctor."

Fear sent her heart pounding faster. "*Nee*, don't go. You know who I am." She wanted to reach for him, but she couldn't move her right arm. Something weighed it down.

"I won't go. I'll stay right here." His voice was calm and reassuring.

Her panic receded. "My name is Mary?"

"Mary Kate Brenneman," he said again.

The nurse injected something into the IV in Mary's arm. "This will help with your pain, Mary Kate. I'm going to inform the doctor you're awake. I'll be right back."

Why didn't her name sound familiar? How could she forget her own name? "I'm Mary Kate Brenneman." If she said it enough, would it feel like it belonged to her? "I'm Mary."

"I've always known you as Mary Kate."

"Can I be plain Mary?" That sounded better somehow.

"All right. You were on your way to stay with my family in New Covenant, Maine when a pickup struck you."

"Maine? That's a long way from Ohio." How could she know that and not remember where she was from?

"It is a long way. You must have been glad to get off the bus."

She didn't remember riding a bus. His face came into focus. She searched it for some shred of familiarity. "You weren't there to meet me."

His expression brightened. "You remember?"

"I heard you say that."

"Oh. I'm sorry I wasn't there, Mary. I should have been."

The door opened and the nurse came back. "The doctor will be in soon. If you want Mr. Fisher to stay, I need your consent to share your medical information. I understand you can't sign this but if you give me your verbal okay that will be enough."

"I guess it's fine." She looked at Ash. He nodded encouragingly.

"Is there anyone we can contact for you? Family? Friends?" the nurse asked.

"I don't know." *Who were they?* She desperately wanted to see a familiar face.

"I'll be back with the doctor shortly." The nurse left the room.

"Would you like a drink of water?" Ash picked up a foam cup from the table beside her bed.

She nodded and took a sip. *"Danki."* She looked at Ash. "Is that right? That means thank you."

"Ja." Ash smiled. "You speak Deitsh—Pennsylvania Dutch the *Englisch* call it."

"I speak Deitsh because I'm Amish." Relief made her light-headed. Or maybe it was the pain medicine. "I'm Amish. I remember that."

"Sell ist goot." He squeezed her fingers.

"You said, 'That is good.' I understand the language but why can't I remember my name or where I'm from?"

"It will come back," he said soothingly.

"Are you sure?"

"If *Gott* wills it. I pray it happens soon."

"I can't seem to move my right arm."

"Because of the cast," Ash said. "Your arm is broken in two places. You have a cracked rib, too."

That explained the pain when she tried to sit up or breathe. Ash gently laid his hand over hers. "You should rest now."

Sleep pulled her toward the darkness. She clutched his hand. "I have so many questions."

"They will keep." His hand slipped from beneath hers.

She missed his touch and struggled to stay awake. "Why was I coming to see you?"

If he replied, she didn't hear.

The welcome darkness wasn't the same this time. Bits and pieces flashed and floated around her. Faces, places. Someone laughing. The sound of weeping. Letters tied together with a ribbon. She struggled to see the flashes more closely, but they drifted away, leaving her alone and frightened in the dark.

Chapter Two

Ash stepped out of Mary Kate's room with a weary sigh. The nurse at the desk beckoned him over. "Dr. Pierre will come speak to you in the waiting room."

He nodded and walked down the hospital corridor to the room at the end of the hall. His parents sat together in one corner.

"How is she?" his mother asked, laying aside her knitting. Ash was glad she was with him. Talitha Fisher had a kind face and a kinder heart.

"She's awake." Should he tell them everything?

"Praise *Gott* for his mercy," Ash's father, Ezekiel, said.

Ash raked a hand through his hair. It was best to share the bad news. "She was awake for a few minutes, but she doesn't know her own name, and she has no memory of her accident or coming to Maine."

"It's called traumatic amnesia." A tall man with a grim expression, graying hair and wearing a white coat stood in the doorway. "It is likely caused by her head injury. I'm Dr. Kevin Pierre."

"She's going to get better, isn't she?" Ash held his breath.

The doctor's grim expression didn't change. "Most episodes of amnesia are temporary, although she might never recall the accident. Her memory may come back the next time she wakes up. Or it may take a few days. She suffered a significant blow to the head."

"What can we do?" Ash's mother asked.

"Have patience. Don't push her to remember. Having familiar sights, sounds and smells may trigger her recall. Let's wait to see how she is when she wakes up again. If you have questions, the staff knows how to contact me. She should do fine."

"*Gott* was watching over her," Ash's mother said. She picked up her knitting. "May I stay with her?"

"Of course, but only two visitors at a time." The doctor left the room.

Ash stopped his mother before she left the waiting room. "She asked to be called Mary, not Mary Kate."

His mother frowned. "Why?"

"I don't know, but if it makes her more comfortable, I don't see the harm."

As Ash's mother went to sit with Mary, Ash took a seat beside his father. "Now what?"

"I'll go home and make sure your brothers are managing."

Ash rubbed his palms on his pant legs. "I should be there, too."

His father shook his head. "*Nee*, you're needed here. I'm sure Mary Kate, Mary, will have questions for you when she wakes. You are the best one to explain her situation."

Ash blew out a breath and leaned back. How could he tell a woman who didn't remember him that she had come a thousand miles expecting to marry him?

Mary woke to the familiar soft beeping again and realized it was beating in time to the throbbing in her head. Another sound caught her attention. It was a subdued clicking noise. She tried to turn to look for it, but the move made her headache worse. She shifted her body trying to find a more comfortable spot, but there didn't seem to be one.

The clicking stopped. "Are you awake at last?" a woman asked in Deitsh.

"I guess I am." Sleep was so much better than

this discomfort, but it was getting harder to re-capture. She noticed the blue sky beyond a window at the foot of her bed. It was daytime but what day? What time was it?

A plump middle-aged Amish woman stepped into Mary's view. She wore a maroon dress with a matching apron and a white *kapp*. She smiled, making laugh lines crinkle at the corners of her dark brown eyes. *"Guder mariye."*

"Is it morning? I can't see well. Do I know you?"

"You do not. I'm Talitha Fisher. You met my *sohn* yesterday. Asher. Do you remember?"

He was the one who knew her. His calm voice had made her first terrifying day bearable. Each time she had opened her eyes, he had been there. "He's been exceedingly kind."

"Do you recall anything else?"

"I was in an accident. I'm in a hospital in Maine. My name is Mary Kate Brenneman. I'm Mary," she said softly. It seemed familiar but still not quite right.

"Wunderbar. What do you remember from before?"

Mary hated looking into the blankness where her life should have been. The pounding in her temples sped up as the emptiness of her past pressed in. The void was too big to be faced alone. She needed an anchor, or it would swallow her. Better to focus on something else. Anything. "Where is your son?"

"He stepped out for a minute."

It was getting hard to breathe. Her chest hurt. Her head pounded. "Ash said he would stay with me. I need to see him."

"All right. I'll get him. He's in the waiting room."

"Please hurry."

Why didn't she know who she was? Who were her parents? What was her mother's name? Who could forget her own mother? Was she married? Did she have children? What did she do in Ohio? What had the bus trip been like to get here? Why had she come? There was nothing. No glimmer of an answer, only frightening emptiness.

She needed to get out of this bed. Swinging her legs over the side, she pushed herself upright. It hurt so much to breathe. She took quick shallow breaths. The room spun. She closed her eyes and felt herself falling.

"Whoa. What do you think you're doing?" Strong hands gripped her shoulders and held her close.

Ash. He was the anchor she needed. She leaned her forehead against his chest until the spinning stopped. She drew a deep breath. His shirt smelled of sun-dried linen and shaving soap.

She saw herself taking a blue work shirt off the

clothesline and holding it to her face to breathe in the scent. Was it a memory?

It vanished before she could be sure.

"Take it easy," Ash said. "Let me help you lie back."

He shifted one arm around her, cradling her head against his shoulder. He slipped his other arm beneath her legs and easily moved her back into bed. She looked up to see his dark eyes brimming with concern. He was wearing a blue shirt today. Her breathing slowed. The pain lessened. "Thank you for staying."

"I said I would." There was an awkward pause as he looked everywhere but at her and rubbed his hands on his pant legs. Finally, he cleared his throat. "Are you okay?"

Her headache had eased. "I'm better now."

"Can I—do something? Can I—get you anything?" He sounded nervous.

"A drink of water."

"Sure." He stepped away from her line of sight. She found she could open her right eye a slit and saw him pouring water from a gray plastic pitcher into a white foam cup. He came back to her bedside and held the straw to her dry, chapped lips. The cold moisture felt wonderful in her mouth and helped soothe her scratchy throat.

"Danki."

He set the cup aside. "Getting up by yourself was not a good idea."

"I won't try it again. I was afraid I might forget you."

A wry smile tipped up the corner of his mouth. "I'm happy you didn't. Have you remembered anything else?"

"Nothing. It's so awful. My life is just gone like it's never been."

The door opened and Dr. Pierre came in, followed by a nurse holding a chart. "Good day, Miss Brenneman. How are you feeling?"

"Worried. My memory is still a blank."

"Don't attempt to force it. It will return on its own."

"You're sure?"

"Very likely. How is your pain level?" He checked her eyes with a small light, listened to her chest and pressed on her tummy. Finally, he straightened. "Nurse, I want her to get up in a chair later." With that, he left the room. The nurse followed him.

Mary looked at Ash. "His bedside manner leaves a lot to be desired. Tell me about myself. How do you know me? Who are my parents? Do I have siblings? Tell me anything. How old am I?"

"All right. Slow down. I know you because we've exchanged letters for several months."

"Like pen pals?"

"*Ja*, like that."

"So we're friends."

"I hope we are. You're twenty-nine. Your parents are deceased. You wrote they died when you were quite young."

"What were their names?"

"Gladys and Peter Hartzler I believe you said in one letter."

"Gladys and Peter." The names meant nothing. "Tell me something else."

"You don't have siblings. You were married. I'm sorry to tell you that your husband died two years ago."

She recoiled. It didn't feel like she had been married, but what did being a wife feel like? "So I'm a widow. What was his name?"

"Edmond Brenneman."

She gripped the blanket and twisted her hand tight in the fold. "I fell in love with Edmond Brenneman and married him." Had she called him Ed or Eddy? How could she forget the man she wed?

"Do I have children?" She braced herself for the answer.

Ash shook his head.

She let out the breath she was holding. That was a good thing. She hadn't forgotten her babies. But she must have loved Edmond. To know she'd forgotten him was almost as painful as forgetting her own life.

Ash cleared his throat. "Do you want to ask me anything else?"

His answers only brought more questions and a deeper sense of loss. "Not right now."

"Okay, I'll be out in the waiting room."

"What? *Nee.* Don't leave. I mean, please stay for a while." She gripped his hand where it rested on the bed rail. He was the only person in the world she had a connection to.

"All right, I'll stay if that's what you want."

He slipped his hand from beneath hers, pulled a chair up to the side of the bed and sat down. Shifting a bit, he rubbed both hands on his pant legs and cleared his throat again.

She wanted to put him at ease. "Tell me something about you."

"Me? There's not much to tell. I'm a dull fellow."

"You're the most exciting man I've met," she quipped.

His eyebrows shot up. "What?"

"I don't know any other men besides you and Dr. Pierre. He's a dull one. He never smiles."

Ash relaxed and grinned. "I'll have to tell my brothers you think I'm exciting and you didn't even see the high-stepping mare I drove to pick you up."

"You have brothers?"

"Three. Gabriel, Seth and Moses. Gabe, Seth and I are triplets. Moses was the Lord's afterthought."

"I don't imagine he likes to hear that. Do you have sisters?"

"Just in-laws. Gabe and Seth married two sisters. Seth's wife is Pamela. Gabe's wife is Esther. She's deaf, and you had planned to learn some sign language before you came. Do you remember any of it?"

"I don't know."

He laid his hand on his chest, then made an *x* with his fingers before making more gestures. "Do you know what I said?"

"None of it looks familiar. What did you say?"

He repeated the signs slowly. "My—name—is—Ash."

"Ash is your nickname?"

"Just about everyone calls me that. Except for Mamm."

"Does she use your middle name when she's upset with you?"

He chuckled. "First middle and last."

"I wish I could remember my mother doing the same. Isn't it strange that I can remember mothers do that, but I can't recall my *mamm* saying it?"

"The doctor said you shouldn't try too hard to remember. It will come back on its own."

"When? I feel like I'm leaning over a huge dark well. I know something is down there, but I can't see it."

"It will happen in *Gott's* time. Until then you have to concentrate on getting better."

"Why did I come here?"

Ash knew she would ask him that. He had already decided on a simplified version of the truth. He thought it best not to mention their possible marriage. It was out of the question until she recovered her memory. The last thing he wanted was for her to feel uncomfortable around him. He would stick with the pen-pal angle because it was true.

"Our community in New Covenant is young. Families only started settling here about four years ago. Our bishop has been seeking more Amish to join us. He was in contact with your bishop who suggested several people who might consider settling here. My family offered to host them, but you were the only one who choose to come. You and I exchanged a few letters so you could gauge what to expect."

Her eyes drifted closed for a moment, then snapped open. "Why did I want to settle in Maine?"

"You wrote that you were looking for opportunities that weren't available in your area. Us not getting many tourists up here appealed to you, too."

"I don't mind the *Englisch*. At least I don't think I mind them."

"We have plenty of *Englisch* neighbors who have welcomed us, but we see few tourists. At least until the Potato Blossom Festival each year."

"You're going to have to explain that." She closed her eyes as her voice grew softer.

"Aroostook County is famous for potatoes. Lots and lots of potatoes grow here."

"I'm not sure if I have forgotten that or if I never knew it." She yawned, then shifted in bed and winced.

He stood up. "You need to get some rest. Have the nurse come get me when you're awake again."

"Don't go. I'm not really sleepy."

"That's why your eyes won't stay open. No arguing, Mary Kate Brenneman," he stated firmly.

She gave him a little half smile. "First, middle and last. I must be in trouble."

"Only if you don't get some rest."

"All right." She sighed deeply and let her head drop back on the pillow.

He headed for the door.

"Ash?"

He stopped and turned around.

"What is your middle name?"

"Ethan."

She closed her eyes again. "Asher Ethan Fisher. I like that. I hope I never have to use all three. Thank you for being my friend."

He smiled. "Sleep well, Mary."

After stepping out, he softly closed the door behind him. He saw Dr. Pierre standing at the nursing station counter and walked toward him. *"Doktah."*

The doctor turned around, looking annoyed at the interruption. "Yes, Mr. Fisher?"

"How long will Mary need to be here?"

"Overall, she's making good progress. Barring any complications, I don't see why she can't convalesce at home. The plan is to discharge her late tomorrow or the day after."

"That soon? What about her memory?"

"As I said, it may take a few days or even a few weeks."

"But it will come back. You're sure?"

"There have been cases where memory loss is permanent, but it's exceedingly rare."

Ash recoiled. "You didn't mention that before."

The doctor's scowl deepened. "I didn't see the point in worrying the patient with a worst-case scenario that is highly unlikely. If there's nothing else, I have rounds to finish." He walked away and went into a nearby room.

Mary was right. Dr. Pierre had a poor bedside manner. Ash continued to the waiting area where his mother was sitting in the corner chair. An *Englisch* gentleman sat watching the television at the other end of the room.

Ash's mother laid her knitting aside. "How is she?"

"Resting now."

"She's very attached to you."

"I think it could be because we've been writing to each other even if she doesn't remember."

"Maybe."

"The doctor said they could discharge her tomorrow or the next day. I imagine she'll want to go home."

"She won't be up to a trip back to Ohio on a bus for weeks. Certainly not alone."

"I thought of that. I know Bishop Schultz has a phone number for her bishop. He can have her family make whatever arrangements work best for them."

"She is welcome to stay with us for as long as she needs. Make sure they know that."

"I will." He pushed out of his chair. "Bishop Schultz should be at his business by now. I'll call him there."

A nurse came into the waiting area. "Mr. Fisher, Miss Brenneman is asking for you."

"I thought she was asleep."

"The police are here to question her. She wants you to be present."

Ash's mother picked up her knitting. "Go on. She needs you. This must be so frightening for her. I'll call the bishop."

"All right." Ash followed the nurse down the hall.

In Mary's room, he found a uniformed police officer standing on either side of her bed. One of them was a woman. The other one was Officer Melvin Peaks Ash had spoken to at the accident. Mary's face was ashen. He stepped closer in concern. "What is it?"

"They want to know if I deliberately stepped into the path of a pickup truck."

He glanced between the two officers in shock. "Why would you ask her such a thing?"

"We found the vehicle," Officer Peaks said. "The driver and his passenger both say Miss Brenneman walked out in front of them. They claim it looked as if she did it deliberately. A suicide attempt."

"What you're suggesting is forbidden." Ash placed his hand on Mary's shoulder. "She did no such thing."

"But you didn't see the accident, did you?" the female officer asked, making notes.

Ash shook his head. "*Nee*. Mary was already

in the ambulance when I arrived. I thought there was a witness."

"When we get conflicting stories, we have to check them out. You don't recall anything from the accident, Miss Brenneman?" Officer Peak asked.

"Nothing before I woke up here."

"Nothing at all? Not how you were feeling? Were you worried or distracted by something?" he prompted.

"I don't remember."

The woman jotted down another note. "We've arrested the driver. He failed to stop and report the accident or call for help. He's facing serious charges even if he wasn't drinking or texting."

Mary shook her head. "It doesn't matter. *Gott* allowed this. I don't want anyone punished. I forgive the driver. Please tell him that."

Her soft-spoken words were what Ash expected. For the Amish, forgiveness always came first.

"It won't be up to you," Officer Peak said.

The female officer finally smiled. "We're sorry this happened. We have your suitcase. It sustained some damage. We'll return the contents as soon as our forensic team has finished with it. We didn't find a purse. Did you have one?"

"I don't know."

Officer Peak looked at Ash. "Would it be un-usual for an Amish woman to travel without a purse or wallet?"

Ash nodded. "It would."

"We didn't find one at the scene." The woman closed her notebook.

"It would be a black bag," Mary said.

Ash squeezed her shoulder. "You remember?"

"I don't, but that is what I would buy. I would choose a black purse."

"We'll keep looking for it. Maybe someone picked it up after the accident and hasn't turned it in yet."

The woman handed Mary a business card. "You can reach us at this number if you recall anything at all. Thank you both for your help."

After the police officers left, Mary massaged her throbbing forehead and then gazed at Ash. She had to ask, but she dreaded hearing the an-swer.

What could have driven her to such desper-ation? "Do you think there is any truth to the driver's claim?"

"None," Ash stated so firmly that Mary had to believe him.

"Why would they say something like that?" What had they seen that made them think she wanted to end her life?

"Only God can see into the hearts of men. Only He can know the answer." Ash cupped her chin and turned her face toward him. "The woman I have been writing to is much too practical and grounded in her faith to consider such a step."

Ash had a way of banishing her fears. She relaxed. "I wish I could meet her."

He gently tapped her forehead with one finger. "She is right in there and she will come out when you least expect her. Remember what the doctor said?"

"I shouldn't try to force myself to remember. It's hard advice to follow." All she could think about was recalling some shred of her former life.

"And you are not great at following advice."

Puzzled, she tipped her head. "What makes you say that?"

"Your in-laws cautioned you not to undertake such an expensive trip."

A new excitement gripped her. "Of course I have in-laws. I was married. What are their names?"

"Edith and Albert Brenneman."

Her excitement faded. The names meant nothing to her. She concentrated on recalling her mother-in-law's face. They had to have been united in their grief. They would have consoled each other. No image came with the name Edith. "Are we close?"

Ash stepped back and looked at his feet. "I got the impression from your letters that there was some friction between you."

Mary frowned. "What kind of friction?"

"You never said."

No matter what had passed between them they were her family. Family was second only to God in importance. "I appreciate you telling me. I'll do my best to mend our relationship as soon as I can."

"I could be wrong."

"I hope so, but if I wrote to you that things weren't *goot* between us, it must be serious. That's not something I would mention casually. I mean, I don't think I would. Do you believe that's why I wanted to come here?"

"Don't fret about it, Mary."

"You're right. I can't mend what's wrong until I remember it, can I?"

"Exactly. Now, you were going to take a nap before the officers arrived. I suggest you finish it."

"I'm tired, but I'm not sleepy. Tell me more about yourself. What do you do? I'm going to take a wild guess and say you raise potatoes."

He chuckled. "A few."

He had a wonderful smile. His dark eyes sparkled when he was amused. She could see the resemblance between him and his mother.

"My family farms, but we are also wheelwrights and buggy makers. My brother Gabriel runs a leather and harness shop. We all help with it, too, especially the women. Gabe's wife is a talented artist. She sells some of her wildflower paintings through a gallery here in Presque Isle."

Mary frowned. "I thought I was in New Covenant."

"That's the name of our settlement. It is much too small to have a hospital or even a post office. Presque Isle is about thirty minutes away by car."

"So your home isn't nearby? Where have you been staying?"

"In the waiting room."

"Where have you been sleeping?"

"In the waiting room."

That surprised her. "Are there beds?"

"There's a bench that isn't too bad."

He'd been sleeping on a bench because she had insisted that he stay with her. She studied his face and noticed for the first time the signs of fatigue around his eyes. "I'm so sorry, Ash."

"For what?"

"For keeping you away from your home and family. Don't tell me your mother has been sleeping here, too?"

"We have an *Englisch* neighbor who has been driving her back and forth."

At least she hadn't disrupted his family completely. "That's how you got a clean shirt. You don't have to stay here anymore, Ash. I'll be fine now. Go home." She swallowed against the tightness that gripped her throat. Her head began pounding as her heart raced. How could she bear this alone?

"Hey, I'm not going anywhere."

"You have a farm and a business to run. You need your sleep as much as I do. Go home. Take a break." She clenched her fingers into a fist.

"Mary, are you sure?"

"I am." He would never know how difficult it was to say those two words.

There was a knock at the door, and his mother looked in. "Asher, I need to speak with you."

"Mary wants us to go home."

She gave Mary an understanding smile. "Then we must do what she asks. She is a grown woman, not a child that needs looking after."

Mary could see his indecision. Finally, he nodded. "You're right. Did you speak with the bishop?"

Talitha's gaze slide away from Mary. "I did. We should let this young woman rest. I'll tell you what he said on our way home."

Mother and son exchanged a speaking glance.

He frowned but turned to Mary with a comforting smile. "I'll see you soon. The hospital has the phone number of our neighbor, Lily Arnett. She will bring us any message and drive me here if I'm needed. Don't worry about bothering us. It's no bother."

"*Danki*, both of you, for all you have done." Her voice started shaking. She stopped talking and turned away. If only they would leave before she began crying. The door closed with a soft click, and she bit down on her bottom lip. There was no reason to be so upset. She had been alone before.

It wasn't a memory. It was a feeling deep in her gut.

Chapter Three

Ash followed his mother to the waiting room. It was empty. He could see she was upset. "What did Bishop Schultz have to say?"

Her frown deepened. She pressed a hand to her chest. "He contacted Mary's bishop the day after her accident."

"I should've known he would." Bishop Schultz would help however he could without being asked. He was a fine man.

"He heard from her family today." Tears welled up in his mother's eyes.

Ash stepped closer. "Mamm, what's wrong?"

"They don't want her back. They're even refusing to help with her medical bills."

He rocked back on his heels. It went against everything the Amish believed. Caring for one another was of paramount importance.

"You can't be serious. Why would they do that?"

"Bishop Schultz is every bit as stunned as we are. She has no other family."

He paced across the room. "I know. She said as much in her letters."

"The bishop spoke to her father-in-law. Asher, her church has shunned her."

He sank onto a chair. "Shunned? For what reason?"

His mother shook her head. "Bishop Schultz doesn't know. Mary Kate's father-in-law wouldn't say anything else."

"Do they understand her condition?"

"Bishop Schultz explained to him about her memory. He said the man was not interested in learning more. He said he would pray for her recovery and hung up. I've never heard of anything like this. It goes against everything our faith stands for to abandon one in such dire need, but the shunning must be the reason."

Ash raked a hand through his hair. "She can hardly repent her transgression if she can't remember what it is. What does the bishop think we should do?"

"He said he must pray about it. To be shunned requires every baptized member of the congregation to agree to it. It is a serious thing. He can't ignore it. He may decide to continue it."

Ash glanced back at Mary Kate's door. "She doesn't need to hear this."

"I agree. We can't tell the poor child that her family won't help her, they don't want her to return and her church has shunned her, but we don't know why. That would be cruel. We must have faith that her memory will return, and she can explain. Was there any hint of this in her letters?"

"She mentioned that there was some friction between herself and her in-laws but nothing else." He couldn't imagine what she had done that would warrant such a drastic step by her church.

"I called Lily Arnett after I spoke to the bishop. She should be here soon to take us home."

"You go ahead. I'm staying."

"Are you sure?"

"I am. She doesn't have anyone." Ash had spent his life surrounded by a loving family. He couldn't imagine facing such a devastating situation alone.

His mother's expression grew concerned. "I will remind you, *sohn*, that you are baptized, and Mary Kate is shunned."

"I can still be a helpful friend."

"That is true. We must pray the bishop decides we can accept her and allow her to join our church. But." She pressed her lips into a tight line.

"But what?"

"Asher, I'm concerned that she didn't share this with you."

"We don't know why. Maybe she intended to tell me in person. Perhaps they have shunned her because she left her own church to join another. A few churches still forbid the practice. Especially if the new group is less conservative."

His mother nodded. "There are too many unknowns in Mary's case. The answers are locked inside her poor, damaged mind."

"She'll get better," he said firmly. "I know she will. In the meantime, I'm responsible for her. She was coming to meet me. If I hadn't dragged my heels leaving home that morning I would have been there when she got off the bus."

"Asher, *Gott* allowed this. We can't know His plan for Mary, but you can't blame yourself."

He could, and he did. "I still feel I must look after her until she can look after herself."

His mother cupped his cheek with her hand. "You are a *goot* boy."

"I had *goot* teachers. I'll be home as soon as I can. Tell those lazy *brudders* of mine to pick up my slack so father doesn't have to do it all."

"They already have. Your *daed* says they are ahead of schedule on the two buggy orders we got last week."

"I hope they're watching the cost of materials. It won't help to rush the work if we are paying more to get it done. Are they keeping good records?" He oversaw the financial side of the family's buggy-building and wheelwright business. His father and brothers were skilled craftsmen, but they sometimes ignored the paperwork that had to be done. He kept the parts inventory stocked, the bills paid and the invoices current. He hated not being there, but he couldn't ignore his responsibility to Mary.

"I'm sure they are. I told Lily I would meet her out front. Are you sure you won't come home for a while?"

"My place is here for now."

"All right. Send word if you need anything or if you change your mind."

After his mother left, Ash told the nurse taking care of Mary where he would be if she needed him, then he went downstairs to find the financial office. Mary would need help to cover the cost of her medical care without a church to take up a collection for her. He had a savings account separate from the business. His father had insisted on that for all his sons. Ash knew he couldn't cover all of Mary's bills, but it would be a start.

He found the woman in the business office familiar with Amish ways and happy to help set up a billing plan for him. She even offered to contact a local charity that provided assistance to the uninsured. He agreed to the help on Mary's behalf. According to her letters, Mary had money of her own, but he had no way of accessing it for her.

He stopped in at the hospital cafeteria next for a quick lunch. He missed his own bed, but he missed his mother's cooking more. The tuna casserole he chose was filling but short on flavor.

Upon his return to the nurses' station, he found Mary's nurse again. "I'm back. I'll be in the waiting room now if she needs me."

"Miss Brenneman became upset after you left. We think she had a panic attack. Dr. Pierre ordered a sedative."

"Is she okay?"

"Yes. She's fine now. She's sleeping. You can go in and sit with her if you like."

"*Danki.* I mean thank you."

"You're welcome."

He pushed open the door slowly and peeked in. The blinds had been drawn. Mary's eyes were closed. He slipped in and sat down beside her.

She looked frail in the dim light and young for her age. He had pictured her as a larger woman from her letters. She'd written about the farm work she did for her in-laws, planting corn and running the harvester alone. The woman in the bed didn't look like she could manage a draft horse team by herself. She was slender and dainty.

The swelling on her face had gone down a little. She was still black-and-blue on her right side, but with her face half turned away he saw how pretty she was for the first time. Her dark brows arched delicately above a small turned-up nose. Her eyelashes rested on her pale cheeks in soft, thick spikes. Her long dark braid flanked the curve of her jaw and the line of her slender neck as it lay over her shoulder and reached past her waist on top of the stark white sheets. He would have to ask what had happened to her *kapp*. She would want her prayer covering when she could get out of bed.

She wore a faint frown as if she was still in pain, even in her sleep. He wanted to smooth the lines away but was afraid his touch might disturb her. He crossed his arms and sat back, content to watch over her as she slept.

The pounding pain in Mary's head came back before she even opened her eyes. She moaned softly, afraid to move and make it worse.

"Shall I get the nurse for you?"

She opened her eyes. Ash sat beside her. A surge of happiness pushed the pain aside. "I thought you had gone home."

"I changed my mind."

"I'm glad."

That was an understatement. She'd never been so glad to see anyone in her life. At least that she could remember. A woman in blue scrubs came in with a tray of food and set it on the bedside table. When she left, Mary watched Ash lift the warming lid and set it aside. "Do you need to sit up higher?"

"I think so." She braced herself for the pain she knew the change in position would elicit as he pushed the button on the bed controller. She clamped her lips together determined not to complain.

He raised the back of her bed slowly. "Is that high enough?"

She nodded and took a shallow breath. It wasn't as bad as she thought it would be. He positioned the table over her lap.

"What made you change your mind?" she asked.

"I was afraid I would miss the hospital cafeteria food."

She stared at the pale chicken over rice and limp green beans. "You're welcome to mine."

"Tempting. But you are the one who needs to get her strength back. Do you take anything in your coffee?"

"Just black." She picked up her fork. "What is this for?"

His perplexed expression was priceless. "Ah, it's called a fork. You eat your food with it."

She started laughing. "I got you with that one."

It took him a second to realize she was teasing him. He grinned and nodded. "You sure did."

Mary took a bite of the green beans. They were as mushy as they looked and bland. She pushed her tray away. "Is your mother still here, too?"

He shook his head. "She went home."

"I'm glad she has some sense. I won't get any rest thinking about you sleeping on a bench in the waiting room tonight." She couldn't get over how sweet he was to someone he had only just met. "Why are you doing this?"

He looked surprised. "You were coming to visit us, and I feel responsible for what happened because I wasn't there to meet you."

"You can't hold yourself to blame." A new thought occurred to her. "Does my family know what happened to me?"

His eyes drifted away from her. "Our Bishop contacted them."

"Are they coming to fetch me?"

"It's a long trip. They have decided that you should stay with my family until you are stronger. Your father-in-law is praying for your speedy recovery."

"I feel if I walked into my home my memory would return, but I guess it's only practical for me to stay awhile. I don't want to be a burden."

He looked back at her and smiled. "I can promise that you won't. My mother would like nothing better than to have you stay with us. The same goes for my sisters-in-law. They were excited to have you stay before the accident. A cast on your arm won't change that."

She turned away from him. "What about an enormous hole where my life should've been?"

"We will do our best to help you recover your memory."

A chill went up her spine. "What if I don't? What if I never remember anything?"

She felt his hand grasp hers. "The doctor says that is highly unlikely."

Gripping his hand tightly, she gazed into his eyes. "But it is possible."

"It is," he admitted reluctantly.

"Then what will I do?"

"Then you will make new memories with me and with my family."

Fear of living with the overwhelming blankness stabbed her through the heart. "I should return to Ohio. My life was there. I need to go back."

"You will when you're strong enough. Until

then you are staying with us." His gaze slid away from her.

Why wouldn't he look at her? Something wasn't right.

Two days later, Mary stepped out of the back of Lily Arnett's car to get her first look at the Fisher farmstead. Set back from the highway on a short gravel lane was a two-story white house with a porch across the front and a well-tended flower garden stretching around the side. Across the farmyard stood a red barn trimmed in white. Attached to the side was a smaller building with a separate entrance and a large multipaned window. A sign over the door said Fisher Harness and Leather Goods. All around and stretching up into the hills was a dense forest. The smell of pine scented the fresh air.

She gazed at the woods in awe. "Look at those beautiful trees."

"Don't they have trees in Ohio?" Ash asked.

"I don't remember. Can I go explore?"

"Maybe in a day or two. You've only just left the hospital."

Looking up at him, Mary sighed, then she grinned. "Ever my practical friend."

"I try."

The front door of the house opened. The Fisher family came out onto the porch. Ash stepped close to Mary's side. She was grateful for his presence. "This is my *daed*, Zeke Fisher, and you know Mamm."

Talitha came down the steps. "Welcome to our home, Mary. I'm sure you must be tired."

"A little," she admitted. This was the longest she'd spent out of bed in almost a week. Her ribs ached from sitting up for the car ride.

"These are my sons. Gabe and his wife, Esther. Seth and his wife, Pamela, and Moses my youngest."

Mary couldn't tell which one was Seth and which one was Gabe as she glanced over their solemn faces. She looked at Ash. "I think you fibbed to me."

"Why would you say that?"

"They don't look like a loud, boisterous bunch." She grinned at his family to take any sting out of her teasing.

Moses cracked a smile. "We can be."

Mary grinned widely. "That's a relief."

"I don't find them loud at all," one of the younger women said with a mischievous glint in her eyes. A smile twitched at the corner of her mouth.

Mary knew she was being teased. She stepped forward and held out her left hand. "You must be Esther. I'm sorry but I seem to have forgotten the sign language I learned."

Esther took her hand in a firm but friendly grip. "We'll teach you all over again."

Mary lifted her cast slightly. "With only one arm?"

"Finger spelling is done with a single hand. It isn't sign language, but I can read it if you can spell it."

"I was an excellent speller in school."

Esther tipped her head slightly. "Were you?"

Mary's bright mood faded. "I don't know why I said that. I can't remember going to school, but I must have. I know how to read."

Talitha took Mary's arm. "You can get better acquainted with us after you've had a rest. Pamela will show you to your room."

Mary nodded and turned to Ash. "My things?"

"I'll bring them in."

The police had delivered the contents of her suitcase in a large cardboard box. The clothes she had been wearing the day of accident were in a plastic bag waiting to be washed.

Mary turned to Lily. "Thank you for driving me here."

"I was happy to do it. If you ever need anything, my place is a short walk through the woods. I'm sure Asher can show you the way."

Pamela came down the steps and hooked her arm through Mary's. "We are so happy you are staying with us."

She led Mary into the house and up the stairs. At the top, a hallway stretched the length of the house. Pamela opened the first door on the left and stepped back to let Mary go in. "I hope this is suitable. You will find the bathroom two doors down on the right."

The room contained two twin beds, both covered with matching bright green-and-white quilts. Pale cream-colored walls were bare except for a wooden rail with pegs to hang clothes on, a calendar with a picture of a snow-covered pine tree and a small mirror over a chest of drawers. A large window with simple white curtains overlooked the flower and vegetable gardens at the rear of the house.

"This is lovely. *Danki.*"

"Goot." Pamela grinned with relief.

"Where do you want these?" Ash asked from the doorway.

"On that bed." She relaxed and pointed.

He put down the box and bag. "Can I do anything else?"

"You have done more than enough for me, Ash. I'm fine."

He smiled with relief. *"Goot.* I've got to get to work in the shop. There's no telling how big a mess my brothers have made of my filing and ordering system."

"Shall I help you unpack?" Pamela asked as she turned down the other bed.

Mary shook her head. "I'll take care of it later."

"That means get out of her hair," Ash said with a wink for Mary.

She grinned. "You know I would never be so rude to anyone but you. Pamela, I need help to put my hair up." She pulled her long braid over her shoulder. "I hate to ask but I can't manage it with one hand."

Pamela pushed Ash out of the room. "I'd be happy to."

When she finished, she pulled down the quilt. "Rest now and we'll see you whenever you feel like coming downstairs."

Mary sank onto the empty bed, but seeing the unpacked box made her get up again. Leaving her work for later didn't seem right. She put her underthings and stockings in the bureau and hung her two good dresses from the pegs, then sat down again. Rubbing her palms on her thighs she looked around. Now what? When she was alone, all she could think about was finding her memory.

There was a knock at the door. Talitha looked in. "I hope I'm not disturbing you."

"Not at all." Mary felt her tension lessen.

"I'm doing a load of laundry and thought I'd ask if you had anything that needed washing."

"My clothes from the day of the accident are in that bag. I'm afraid they're a mess."

"With four sons I am used to messes." Talitha picked up the plastic bag. She turned to Mary with a sympathetic smile. "I know this must seem strange, but keep in mind that you were coming to visit us. We have been expecting you for days. I enjoy having company so never think you are putting me out."

Mary drew a shaky breath. She tried to maintain her usual smile, but her lower lip quivered. "I'm so grateful for all you and your family have done. If it weren't for Ash sitting with me for hours in the hospital, I don't know how I would have made it this far. The truth is I'm scared."

"Of what?"

"What if I don't want to remember because I was a horrible person?" Tears welled up and spilled down her cheeks. She couldn't hold back a sob.

Talitha sat beside Mary and put her arm around her. "Go ahead and cry. I can't imagine what you're going through. Just remember that our Lord is beside you, too. His comfort is the greatest of all."

Mary nodded because she couldn't speak. The dread and fear of not knowing choked her. Ash would drive back the darkness if only he were here.

* * *

Ash was in the living room with the family when his mother came downstairs. "How is she?"

"Exhausted. Frightened half out of her mind. She may not remember anything, but I can tell she is a dear, sweet girl. I find it hard to forgive her family for turning their backs on her."

"We don't know the circumstances of her shunning," Zeke said.

Ash's mother planted her hands on her hips. "She has cried herself to sleep. I don't care about the circumstances. We're going to make her feel welcome and treat her as a valued member of our family for as long as she wishes to stay."

Ash saw a smile twitch at the corner of his father's mouth. "I wasn't suggesting otherwise, but the bishop has the final say."

"I'm aware of that," she admitted.

"We must obey the Ordnung," he said sternly.

"Of course. Esther and Pamela, can you take care of lunch?" She signed as she spoke for Esther's benefit.

"What will we do about Mary?" Pamela asked. "The church forbids us to eat at the same table with a shunned person."

"Our table is already crowded with all of us around it. Too crowded to squeeze in one more. We need a bigger table." Ash's mother shot a stern look at her husband.

"I'm going to build a new one soon," he said.

She rolled her eyes. "I've heard that before. We'll seat Mary by herself at a card table so no one accidentally jars her broken arm, and we will adhere to our Ordnung at the same time."

"A *goot* idea." Pamela smiled and followed Esther into the kitchen.

"The buggy won't finish by itself." Ash's father started toward the door. His sons followed.

"Asher, may I speak to you for a moment?" His mother sat on the sofa.

"I should have a look at the books," Ash said. "I've neglected them long enough."

She patted the cushion beside her. Ash grimaced at another delay. "Mamm, I need to get back to work. Those brothers of mine will have made a mess of the paperwork, and I'm days behind on ordering parts."

"This won't take long. You've devoted a lot of time to Mary and she's grateful."

He sat down and propped his elbows on his knees. "So?"

"I'm worried about her. She's in a very frail state."

"I understand that."

"Not just physically. She's lost, alone, worried. This has made her dependent on you."

"I know that, but now that she's here with you,

Pamela and Esther I'm sure she'll be fine. The business needs me, too."

"I believe you should let your brothers continue taking over your work in the shop for a few more days so you can devote your time to Mary. Until she is comfortable here. I believe that will help more than anything."

Astonished by her suggestion, he blinked hard. "You want me to spend more time with a woman the bishop may tell us we must shun?" He couldn't deny he was drawn to Mary, but nothing could be the same between them now.

"She came here because you invited her, Ash."

He clapped a hand to his chest. "And I felt responsible for her in the hospital, but now she has you she can turn to."

"All I'm asking is for you to continue your friendship with the poor girl. I'll tell your brothers and your father what I've decided." She patted his knee, rose and walked out leaving Ash's mind reeling. What was she thinking?

Chapter Four

Mary opened her eyes in a strange room. It took a moment to remember she was in Ash's home instead of the hospital. She sat up gingerly and rubbed her temple. Crying always left her with a headache, but she couldn't remember a time when she had wept in the past.

She must have if she had buried a husband. What kind of person could forget that sorrow? What kind of person was she? Looking out over the garden, she saw Talitha hanging out her washing.

The image of holding a sun-dried blue work shirt in her hands flashed into Mary's mind. She held the shirt to her face and breathed in the smell, and she wanted to weep.

She had cried over that shirt. Why? Whose was it? She tried but couldn't recall anything else. The memory was real. She was sure of it.

Maybe this meant the doctor was right, and she was recovering. She should tell Ash.

She rushed from the room and went downstairs. Ash and his father sat at a desk in the living room, intent on the papers spread in front of them. Suddenly it seemed foolish to be so excited over taking a piece of clothing off the line. She must have done it hundreds of times.

Ash looked up. "Are you feeling better?"

"I am. *Danki.*" Would it sound foolish to say she recalled holding a shirt?

He tipped his head slightly. "What is it?"

"Nothing. Well, maybe. I think I remembered something."

He jumped to his feet and hurried to her side. "That's *wunderbar.*"

She blushed and looked down. "It isn't much."

"Tell me."

"I took a man's work shirt off the line and held it to my face. I wanted to cry. That's all."

"Who did it belong to?"

She shrugged and looked at him. "I don't know."

"Perhaps it belonged to your husband," he said gently.

"I reckon that's the most likely answer. It was just a flash but I'm sure it is a memory. I said it wasn't much." Feeling foolish, she turned away.

He gripped her hand and bent his face to look into her eyes. "It's a start, Mary."

She liked the way his voice softened when he said her name. It made her feel special and safe.

Ash's father came to stand beside them. "You must be hungry. You slept through lunch."

"I am a little."

"She's been eating like a bird in the hospital," Ash said.

His father smiled at her. "I'm sure there's something for you in the kitchen. Ash, why don't you show her the way."

She shook her head. "Don't let me take you from your work."

"We're done." Ash looked at his father who nodded. "The kitchen is this way."

He led her through a doorway into a spacious, sunny room with a large oak table in the center that had a card table on the end. A row of windows above the sink and counters were open to the breeze. A coffeepot sat on the back of a huge black stove. Ash walked to the icebox and opened it. "Chicken or ham?"

"Ham. What's the card table for?"

"It's for you. Mamm wanted you to sit where no one will bump your arm," he said in a rush. "It's crowded with all of us at meals. Mamm had been asking for a bigger table for ages, but Daed hasn't gotten around to making one."

"That's thoughtful." Mary took a seat at the little table while he supplied her with a plate, bread, mustard and a plastic container of sliced meat. She built herself a sandwich. It wasn't until she took the first bite that she realized how hungry she was.

He took a seat across from her and watched her intently. She grew nervous under his scrutiny. "What?"

"You have some mustard on the side of your mouth."

"That's because I'm eating like a pig." She wiped her hand over her lips. "Did I get it?"

"Not quite." He reached across the table, curled his fingers under her chin and brushed his thumb gently across the corner of her mouth.

Her breath caught. A wave of heat rushed to her cheeks. She pulled away and rubbed her face with the back of her hand. Glancing at him, she saw a puzzled expression darken his eyes. He raked his fingers through his hair and got up to fix himself a cup of coffee. He leaned against the counter to sip it.

She concentrated on taking smaller bites and tried not to think about the rush of delight his touch triggered. It had been a simple, helpful gesture. He was only being friendly. They knew each other well enough for that. It was her response that was out of proportion. She prayed he hadn't noticed. He took a seat across from her.

When she finished her meal, she picked up her plate and carried it to the sink. She washed and rinsed it, using the time to regain her composure. She turned around with a bright smile. "Now what? Do not say rest because I have spent far too much time doing that already."

He turned toward her and hooked one arm over the back of his chair. "I'm willing to hear a reasonable suggestion."

"Can we take a walk in the woods?"

"A short one."

She raised one eyebrow. "Define short."

"Ten minutes."

"Thirty."

He arched his brow to mimic her. "Fifteen."

"Fifteen with the possibility of five more if I'm not tired?"

He inclined his head slightly. "If you promise you won't overdo it. I don't want to have to carry you back to the house."

It was easy to visualize being held in his arms. She ruthlessly pushed the image aside before she started blushing. "I will tell you the minute I start to fade."

He got out of his chair, lifted his hat from the row of pegs beside the door and held it open. She scooted through, making sure she didn't touch him. Outside, she surveyed the woodlands that curved around the property. "It is so beautiful here."

"It looks a lot different in the winter."

"Do you get much snow?"

"Six feet or more."

"Feet? The snow piles up higher than my head?" It was hard to believe, but what a wondrous sight it must be.

"Yup. Sometimes higher."

"Oh, I wish I stay here to see that."

He frowned. "Why won't you be here?"

"Because I'm going back to Ohio as soon as the doctor says I'm strong enough to travel. My family must be worried about me. I'll write them tomorrow if someone will help me."

"Of course we will."

When she was at home among familiar people and places her memory would return if it didn't before then. She prayed it would come back soon.

Pushing her worry aside, she glanced around. "What fun the winters must be here. Do you go sledding? You must with such wonderful hills."

"I do lots of shoveling, and I chop tons of wood."

"But surely you go ice skating and take sleigh rides. Do you ski?"

"I don't. Moses like to. There's a path behind

the barn that leads up to a meadow with a pretty view from the top. Shall we go there?"

Her arm ached, but she ignored it. She didn't want to miss a minute of being outside in Ash's company. "Lead on."

Ash walked beside Mary without speaking. He was still coming to grips with the sudden jolt of emotion that had blindsided him in the kitchen when he touched her face. His boldness had shocked her. He could tell that much. Determined not to repeat his mistake, he kept his hands clasped around his suspenders so he wouldn't accidentally touch her.

Her comment about going back to Ohio had caught him off guard, too. Should he tell her about her family's decision? He hated keeping it from her but decided to wait.

As they made their way along the path into the deep woods, she gazed about in childlike wonder, asking him the names of the birds that flitted through the canopy overhead. He knew most of them. His brother Gabe was an avid birdwatcher. He had educated everyone in the family on the different birds in the area, whether or not they were interested.

She stopped suddenly. "Oh, look," she whispered, her voice full of awe.

He followed her line of sight and saw a fox.

What was so amazing about that? They were plentiful.

"She has two babies with her." She kept her voice low.

"They're called kits," he said in his normal tone. The fox bolted at the sound of his voice.

Mary frowned at him. "You scared them away."

"They won't go far. You might see them another time. We'll have to make certain to lock up the hens and geese at night."

"Do fox do a lot of damage?"

"They're good at keeping the rodent population in check but not everyone believes that. They are hunted around here."

"What a shame. They're pretty."

Mary kept walking but soon stopped to rub the bark of an old oak. "Moss grows thick on the north side of the trees here."

A squirrel took exception to their presence and began scolding from the branches. She looked up at him. "I like your home."

She leaned in to smell the moss and smiled with her eyes closed. "I think this is exactly what I imagined a forest in Maine would be like. A dim, welcoming place full of earthy scents. Quiet in a reverent way, except for the rustling of wildlife and the sound of the wind in the branches.

Like *Gott* had just breathed it to life. Did you describe it like that in your letters to me?"

"Nee." He didn't think of the woods as anything special. They were just trees. He never suspected from her letters that Mary had a fanciful imagination.

Stepping back, she smiled shyly. "Am I being silly?"

He thought it best not to answer. "These woods have many practical uses. The forested acres were part of the reason we purchased this property. We heat our house with the logs we cut so we don't have to buy propane. Some of the timber like this big tree will be logged off and sold to the local lumber mill to supplement the income from the farm and our businesses."

Her grin faded as she looked up. "You mean to cut down this tree? Mr. Squirrel will miss his home."

He frowned. "Taking a few of the older trees gives more room for the young ones that get crowded out. We can earn a small income and still manage the land responsibly. One of our neighbors is a logger. Nathan Weaver. He's Amish, and he'll use his horses. That way we won't have to clear a way for a road."

"I guess that's okay. It is just sad to cut down something so magnificent."

"People need wood for houses and businesses."

"I reckon that's a practical way to look at it."

"Right," he said with relief. There was the realistic Mary he knew from her letters.

She looked up again. "You may have to move to a new house, Mr. Squirrel."

The animal continued to scold them. Mary grinned at Ash. "He doesn't like that idea. Perhaps you can convince him."

Talking to squirrels wasn't how Ash normally spent his time. "Are you getting tired?"

She frowned at him. "Don't say we have to go back. Not yet." There was pleading, but also a hint of panic in her voice.

"We can go a little farther," he said to mollify her.

"*Wunderbar.* You are my hero." Her beaming smile made his heart catch. He closed his hands tightly around his suspenders to keep from reaching for her hand.

She wasn't what he'd expected. From her correspondences, he assumed they would get along well together, but this attraction was different. Confusing. How could she make him giddy with a simple smile? He forced his attention to the path ahead. "Don't overdo it."

The trail led upward into the wooded hills above New Covenant. There were several breaks in the trees with fine views of the distant mountains and the winding river below.

They stopped at one opening in the trees where the valley lay spread out in a checkered patchwork of fields and farms. She smiled at him. "Ash, this is beautiful."

He cocked his head slightly. It was a pretty view. "Esther and Pamela say the clearing beyond those cedar trees is their favorite spot."

"Then I must see it."

He led her around the trees and noticed her steps were slowing. He'd brought her too far. Luckily, there was a place to rest up ahead.

The clearing they reached held the ruins of an old log cabin sitting amid a carpet of pink, lavender, purple and white spires of lupine. His brother Gabe had built a bench where Esther could sit and sketch the flowers.

Mary gasped and stepped out into the meadow with a delighted smile. She held out her good arm and turned in a circle. "They're beautiful. I've never seen anything like it."

Her smile faded as her eyes grew sad. "I say that, but I can't be sure it's true."

He wanted her to smile again. "It's true today."

"You're right." She pressed a hand to her temple and sat on the bench. "Thank you for showing me this. I reckon we should go back, but I don't want to."

"This will be here tomorrow and the next day. You can come again."

"It's not that." She rubbed her shoulder and adjusted her sling.

He sensed her unease and sat beside her. "Why don't you want to go back?"

She averted her gaze. "Everyone will stare at me, much too polite to say anything, but wondering what kind of ninny can't remember her own name."

He brushed the backs of his fingers lightly across the bruise that still marred the side of her face. "*Nee*, they won't. My family will think how blessed you are to have survived such a terrible accident."

When she looked at him, tears glistening in her eyes. "You're very kind, Ash."

"I thought I was the most exciting man you know. Now I'm only kind. It seems I'm slipping in your estimation." He couldn't believe he was teasing her.

She managed a wry smile. "I don't want to puff you up."

"I see. This is you keeping me from becoming prideful, is it?"

"Exactly."

"You're doing a fine job. Let's get you home before Mamm scolds us both for keeping you out too long."

"I didn't mean I thought your family would be unkind."

"I know that."

"When I think about the missing part of my life, I feel empty and scared."

"I can fill in a few things for you. I wish I had kept your letters. They might have helped."

"How did I seem? Was I a cheerful person, or did I worry over things?"

"I got the feeling that you were unhappy with your in-laws."

"Did I write about my friends and the things we did together?"

"You mentioned going to a church social and a frolic. Mostly you wrote about work on your father-in-law's farm. You didn't mention specific friends."

"What did I do for fun?" she asked eagerly.

"I couldn't say."

Her expression dimmed. "Oh, well, that's okay."

"I'm not much help, am I?"

"Of course you are, Ash." Her earnest tone soothed his failure. "Why, if not for you I still wouldn't know my name. You've been loads of help. I've been praying that my memory returns. Maybe I should pray for patience instead."

"Pray for both." He took her hand to help her to her feet.

Mary was prepared for his touch this time. She didn't pull away but allowed her hand to linger in his strong one for a moment longer than necessary. The same surge of awareness flowed through her veins bringing a bewildering happiness. She liked Ash Fisher. Everything about him pleased her. The color of his eyes, the shape of his lips, the strength in his hands. She especially liked the way he always tried to comfort her.

He nodded toward the path. "We should go."

She realized she was staring at him and began walking. Had she felt this way when she was with the husband she couldn't remember? What had he been like? Did Ash remind her of him in some way? Did they act or look alike? Did she still mourn him? Was that why she was attracted to Ash? Her somber thoughts took the joy out of her walk. She shifted her arm again. It was aching dreadfully and so was her side.

"You've gotten quiet," Ash said.

"I'm afraid I overdid it. My arm hurts." Her headache was back, too.

"Do you want to stop and rest?"

"*Nee*, let's keep going. It isn't far now and it's downhill."

He stopped. "I can carry you."

"Oh, *nee*, that won't be necessary." She picked up the pace and moved ahead of him so he couldn't see how flustered his suggestion made her. He might know her, but she barely knew him. She didn't even know if he had a girlfriend.

That thought brought her up short. He stopped beside her. "What?"

"Nothing." She started walking again. There was no way she was going to ask him such a pointed and personal question.

They emerged from the trees a short time later. She stopped at the front door and turned to him with her chin up. "Thank you for accompanying me on a walk. You have a lovely place. I'm going in now. You should return to your work. I've kept you from it long enough."

Was her tone casual enough? Please let him think so.

"Okay." He looked perplexed.

After opening the door, she slipped inside, closed it and leaned against the cool wood. Why hadn't she considered he might be seeing someone before? He had been attentive to her, but he felt guilty about the accident. That was the reason he was so considerate. Imagining it was something else was a mistake. Until she could remember her past life, she had no business thinking about any kind of relationship with Ash. She had no idea what kind of person she was, what troubles might have prompted her to want to move to Maine.

She liked Ash, but she couldn't continue this dependence on him. He had been there in the beginning when she desperately needed someone, but she was better now. Her memory might be missing, but her strength of will wasn't. It had been badly bent under the overwhelming fear of those first few days, but it was time to straighten it out.

She pushed away from the door. What she needed was to be useful. She went in search of her hostess and found her with Pamela and Esther in the kitchen. They all looked at her when she walked in.

Pasting a smile on her face, she advanced into the room. "I need something to do. Put me to work and don't any of you dare tell me to go rest."

There was an awkward silence in the kitchen. Mary met their gazes without flinching. Having only one arm, a cracked rib and a splitting headache would not deter her.

Esther gestured for Mary to sit at the table. "I'm making cupcakes. Why don't you fill these liners with batter while I start on another batch?"

Mary gave her a grateful smile. "I can manage that. How do I say *danki* in sign language?"

Esther brought her fingers to her lips and extended them to Mary. "This is how you say thank you."

Mary repeated the gesture with a smile for the understanding woman, sat down and began working. While she filled the cupcake liners, she found her mind wandering. To Ash and the way he made her feel today. She wanted to spend more time with him, get to know him better and see where this attraction might lead, but that wasn't possible. She had to ignore those feelings.

"Are you finished with these?" Talitha asked pointing to the pan in front of Mary.

Mary looked up. "Sorry. Guess I was lost in thought."

"Something serious by your expression. Can I help?"

"I was thinking I've been a burden to Ash since the accident. He's such a kind man he'd never admit it."

Talitha tipped her head as she regarded Mary. "Asher thinks more highly of you than you realize."

Mary forced herself to smile. "He has proven to be a true friend."

Ash entered the part of the barn his family used for making buggies and wheel repair with a deep sense of relief. He was more than ready to get back to work and forget how confused Mary made him feel. He didn't even get the door closed behind him before Seth rolled out from underneath the half-completed buggy frame. "You sure landed yourself in a pickle, *brudder*."

Gabe came through the door that connected to

his leather shop. "You poor fellow. Your bride-to-be has finally arrived, and she doesn't know you. Is she what you expected?"

Looking at the grins on his brothers' faces made Ash glare at them. "That's hardly a fair question."

"Oh, I reckon you're right," Seth admitted. "How is she feeling?"

"Better physically, but mentally she's having a hard time coming to grips with her situation."

"Can't blame her for that," Gabe said. "What about you?"

"Me? I feel pretty much the same. We aren't exactly strangers. I thought I knew her. We've been corresponding for months but none of that exists for Mary. She certainly isn't like I imagined. We took a walk up into the forest. You have never seen someone so delighted to be among trees. She was even talking to a squirrel. When I mentioned the logging we planned to do in that area, I thought she was going to cry. Her letters made her sound much more down-to-earth. I'm not sure if the difference is because of the accident or if I don't know her as well as I thought I did. Can we just get to work?"

"Such a serious injury is bound to have a profound effect on her," Gabe said.

Ash nodded. "I expect you're right."

Seth stroked his short beard. "We're worried

about you, Ash. Gabe and I know you better than anyone. The three of us are all for one and one for all, remember? This sudden rush into a long-distance courtship isn't like you. We're concerned you are doing it for the wrong reason."

"What reason is that?" Ash asked with a degree of caution.

Gabe laid a hand on Ash's shoulder. "We think our marriages have you feeling left out and maybe lonely."

Ash shouldn't be surprised his brothers knew him so well. "Is it wrong to want what the two of you have? A loving wife and a chance to start my own family? There isn't anyone around here for me. I can't leave the business to go shopping for a wife in another community. I've done the numbers. We're finally getting ahead, but one bad potato harvest or someone canceling a buggy order will be enough to undo all our hard work. The move here and this business is our father's dream. We can't fail him. When the bishop suggested I exchange letters with some single Amish women looking to relocate with an eye toward marriage, it seemed like a good solution. And it was."

"Why Mary?" Gabe asked.

Ash shrugged. "She was a widow in an unhappy situation with her in-laws, looking for a chance to start over. Her letters said she wasn't expecting a love match, but she believed two practical people could work together to form a lasting relationship. She was desperate to start a new life."

"You felt sorry for her," Seth stated.

"A little. She didn't have high expectations, which suited me."

He turned and took a few steps away. "You know how I am around women. I trip over my tongue the second I open my mouth. It just seemed like the easiest way to get what the two of you have. I know you must think this makes me pathetic."

Seth walked up and punched Asher's shoulder. "You've been pathetic since the day you were born. This doesn't change anything."

Ash rubbed his arm. "Leave it to you to make me feel better."

Gabe punched Seth in the shoulder. "Pointing out someone else's faults does not lessen your own. If not for Ash's way with numbers, our businesses would still be in the red."

"True," Seth admitted. "But if Mary is simply looking for a practical fellow to get her away from her unhappy life and provide nothing more than companionship, she isn't the woman for you, Ash. You deserve to find the love of your life. Someone you can't live without."

"Someone who makes you feel like you can't breathe when they're near," Gabe said softly.

Ash saw the concern in his brothers' eyes. What they spoke of was what he wanted. Had he been foolish to think he could settle for less?

Seth sighed. "When her memory returns, you will have to be honest and tell her that you are looking for a love match."

Ash swallowed hard. "There is one problem with that. When Mary regains her memory, she's going to recall I have already asked her to marry me."

Chapter Five

"What?" Gabe's mouth dropped open. "You proposed to Mary?"

"In my last letter to her." If only he hadn't mailed that brief spur-of-the-moment note. Nothing good came from impulsive decisions.

"What was her answer?" Seth demanded.

"I assumed she would tell me when she arrived."

"So you don't know if you're betrothed or not?" Gabe asked.

"Unless she tells me otherwise, I have to assume I am."

Seth lifted his hat and raked his hand through his blond hair. "No wonder you looked so worried the morning you went to meet the bus. I'm sorry I teased you about it. I thought she was coming for a visit to get to know you and the community."

"That was our original plan, but then I sent that last letter."

"What are you going to do now?" Gabe asked.

"I'm sure Mamm told you Mary is shunned." They nodded.

"I have no idea what to do." Ash folded his arms and looked down. "I pray the bishop gives us an answer quickly."

Gabe took a few steps away then turned around to face Ash. "Bishop Schultz is a wise and kind man. He'll see shunning her accomplishes nothing until we know the full story. Mary's injury is giving her a chance to get to know Asher Fisher without her preconceived notions. You are learning who she is when she isn't a desperately unhappy widow hoping marriage will solve her troubles. She's already seen how compassionate you are. I know you didn't tell her that in a letter."

"Of course not. I wrote about practical everyday things. So did she."

Gabe smiled. "I'm not sure a fellow as practical as you claim to be would have stayed by her bedside day and night. You've known her a few days now. Do you like her?"

Ash wasn't willing to share how Mary affected him. Those feelings were still new and confusing. "She was alone and needs someone to look after her. The whole thing was my fault. I wasn't there to meet her bus."

"She's not alone now," Seth said.

"I'm the one person who knows something about her. I'm her only friend. She depends on me."

His brothers exchanged speaking looks. Gabe drew a deep breath. "I want an honest answer, Ash. Do you feel compelled to befriend Mary because you feel guilty? Or is it because you like her?"

Ash turned away from his brothers. "Does it matter?"

"Does it matter?" Gabe's voice boomed throughout the workshop. Ash flinched.

"*Ja*, it matters a lot," Seth said. "You can't build a lasting relationship based on guilt and pity."

Ash spun to face them. "It's my life. I'll handle it. You both must promise you won't mention any of this to Mary. I don't want her upset."

"Of course we won't," Seth said. "Do Mamm and Daed know about this?"

"That I proposed? *Nee*, I haven't told anyone. They think Mary has come to see if she wants to move here, but they know we've been writing to each other. Mamm may suspect we have formed an attachment. She always has matchmaking on her mind."

Gabe grinned at Seth. "We're proof she knows what she's doing. If she and her cousin Waneta hadn't cooked up a reason to bring Esther and Pamela here for a visit, we'd still be single men."

Seth's eyes narrowed. "Do you think that's what she's doing now?"

Ash frowned. "What do you mean?"

"She told us to keep working without you because Mary wasn't comfortable with you out of her sight. Our mother always makes people feel welcome and happy. If anyone can make Mary comfortable here without a second thought, it's her."

Gabe nodded. "You're right."

Ash shook his head. "*Nee*, Mamm wouldn't do such a thing unless Mary had rejoined the faith."

Gabe held up one hand. "I'm not so sure. She knows fallen-away Amish have come back because of love. *Gott* uses many tools to lead His children to Him."

Seth stroked his beard thoughtfully. "If Mamm is intent on matchmaking, she'll see that you two spend more time together. She has her ways. You and Mary have a connection you felt was serious enough to propose marriage, but you don't really know her. Spending time with her is the only way you can decide if she's the right one or not. If she isn't, she deserves to hear the truth from you."

Ash was tired of talking about it. "Until her

memory returns, I'm a helpful friend and nothing more. Now, I need to look at the ledgers. Did either of you do inventory while I was gone?"

Seth shrugged. "Daed was going to, but it's been busy here."

Ash shook his head in disgust. "I knew this would happen."

The outside door opened. Pamela looked in. "Ash, Talitha would like you to change the propane tank in the end table beside the living room sofa. It's not working."

He struggled to contain his annoyance at another delay. "Where is Moses? Why can't he do it?"

"I don't know. Your mother specifically asked for you to take care of it. I'm just the messenger. Mary wants to read a book, but the lamp won't turn on."

"Okay, I'll be right there." Pamela left, and Ash heard snickering behind him. He spun around to see his brothers trying not to laugh.

"I told you Mamm has her ways," Gabe said. "Don't bother hauling a new tank in. I changed that one yesterday and it was working fine."

Ash went out and slammed the workshop door shut on the sound of their guffawing. He paused and drew a calming breath before he entered the house. In the living room, Mary sat on the sofa with her feet up on the ottoman and her broken arm elevated on a stack of pillows. A blue quilt covered her lap.

She looked at him and frowned. "Is something wrong?"

"Nee."

"You look annoyed."

"Sorry. Work stuff. Nothing I should burden you with. What seems to be the trouble?"

"I am. Your *mamm* insisted I rest here and read or something because I refuse to go back to bed. I'm no use in the kitchen with one hand. Pamela and Esther kindly made sure I'm comfy with these pillows and throw. They are determined to spoil me. Talitha tried to light the lamp, but the tank seems to be empty."

He opened the small door on the front of the oak end table to check. He saw right away that the valve had been turned off. "It's not empty. Someone shut the valve."

"I wonder why she didn't see that?"

"I'm afraid to guess." He should tell his mother he didn't need her matchmaking help.

Mary gave him a funny look. "What?"

"Never mind." He twisted it to the On position and stood up. Using the lighter that was always kept on the table, he lit the mantle inside the glass globe. Bright white light flooded the dim corner of the room. "Better?"

"Much." She smiled and picked up her book.

He had work waiting, but he surprised himself by sitting beside her feet on the ottoman. "What are you reading?" The book had a plain blue cover jacket on it.

"Esther gave it to me. She said she really likes this author. I don't think I've read anything by her before, but I'm sure I like love stories."

Ash felt his face growing warm. "Then I will let you get back to it."

She laid the book aside. "*Nee*, I'd rather visit with you. Unless you're busy."

"Nothing that can't wait. Is your arm hurting?"

She grimaced and flexed her fingers. "A bit."

"Are you regretting our hike in the woods?"

"Absolutely not. It was amazing. Much better than cornfields." A small furrow appeared between her eyebrows. "I don't know why I said that."

"I might. You wrote about planting and harvesting corn on your father-in-law's farm in Ohio. You tried to convince him to hire another farmhand to make the job easier, but he wouldn't."

"I worked as a farmhand on my father-in-law's property?" She tipped her head. "I'm trying to visualize that."

"You frequently drove a four-horse hitch for him. That takes a lot of muscle." He glanced at her slender arms and dainty hands.

"I wish I could remember."

"Nothing has occurred to you since this morning?"

"I would say I'm still in the dark, but you just fixed the lamp." She giggled. "That was a poor joke, wasn't it?"

"Not poor, just silly."

Her eyes widened. "If that's the way you're going to be I'm done visiting with you." She lobbed one of her pillows at him.

He caught it and tossed it back. "*Goot.* I have work to do."

She replaced the pillow under her cast. "Don't let me keep you."

He rose and started for the door and saw his mother watching from the hallway. She gave a knowing smile and went into the kitchen.

"Ash?"

He looked back at Mary.

She brought her fingers to her lips and extended her hand to him. "For fixing the light."

From Esther it felt like the sign for *thank you*. From Mary, it reminded him of someone blowing a kiss. Was she flirting? No, he had to be mistaken, but he was glad his mother hadn't seen it.

"You're welcome." He hurried out the door and escaped into his small office in the workshop. He opened his ledger and stared at the numbers without really seeing them.

Mary loved trees, talked to animals, made silly jokes, threw pillows at a fellow and she might have been flirting. He had been drawn to Mary's serious, down-to-earth nature in her letters. The woman in the house didn't fit what he knew about her, yet she was remarkably appealing. Spending more time with her wouldn't be a hardship. He smiled at the thought.

Then his common sense made him sit up straight. She was shunned. Until the bishop decided whether to support the shunning of another community, Ash couldn't allow his attraction to get out of hand. He could be pleasant and helpful, a friend. Nothing else.

He heard hoofbeats outside his office and rose to look out the window. Otto Gingrich, a young boy from New Covenant, sat on a spotted pony talking to Ash's father and mother. Ash went to see what was up.

Otto wheeled his pony around and trotted away. Ash saw the concerned look his parents shared as he reached them. "What's going on?"

"The bishop sent word," his father said. "He'll be here to speak to Mary in the morning."

Mary struggled to get her *kapp* pinned on straight the next morning. A knock at her door interrupted her efforts. "Come in," she mumbled around the bobby pin in her mouth.

Talitha opened the door. "I came to see if you needed help to dress."

Mary held out the bobby pin. "I've managed everything but my prayer covering."

Talitha took the pin, straightened the *kapp* and secured it in place. "There. Now you look ready to face the day. Have you remembered anything else?"

Mary didn't bother to hide her disappointment. "I haven't."

"Never mind. All in *Gott's* own time. There is someone downstairs who would like to meet you. Bishop Schultz is here."

"I must thank him for letting my family know about me." She expected to meet him at the church service, but she wasn't surprised he had come beforehand. She was an oddity. A woman with no memory. The Fisher family could probably expect to have a steady stream of visitors over the next week.

She chided herself for being cynical. Ash's family hadn't made her feel like a freak. "What is he like?"

"I think you will like him. He's a potato farmer, but he also owns a shed-building business. He makes tiny houses and log cabins now, too. His sermons are sometimes rambling, but he is a fair man, well-liked in our community and respected by our *Englisch* neighbors."

Mary followed Talitha downstairs. The man was seated on the sofa between Ash and Zeke. They got to their feet when the women came into the room. Ash had a worried expression on his face.

"Mary, this is Elmer Schultz. He is our bishop," Zeke said.

Bishop Schultz was an imposing man who looked be in his late fifties or early sixties. His shaggy gray-and-black beard reached to the middle of his black vest. His gray hair showed the indented impression of his hat around his head. "How are you, Mary?"

She cradled her cast and kept her eyes down. "Improving thanks to the care and kindness of the Fisher family."

"I'm glad to hear that. Please, take a seat."

The straight-backed chair had been set in front of the sofa. A trickle of unease went down her spine. She sat down. Talitha stood behind her.

"I have a few questions for you. Is it your intention to practice the Amish faith here in New Covenant?"

That surprised her. "Of course. I may have forgotten my name but not my faith in *Gott*."

"Do you offer forgiveness to those who have harmed you?"

Was he talking about the driver of the truck that hit her? "Absolutely."

"What if you have knowingly or unknowingly harmed someone?"

Mary grew increasingly puzzled by his questions. "I would seek their forgiveness and try to make amends."

"If you could leave our faith for any reason, would you do that?"

She frowned. "I would not. I have made my vows to *Gott* and the church."

"Do you remember doing so?"

If only she could. "*Nee*, but I was married so I must have been baptized."

He nodded slightly to Zeke. "I'm satisfied."

Facing Mary again, he folded his hands together. "As you have been told, I notified your bishop of the accident, and he informed your family. Your father-in-law called me two days later. This is going to be hard for you to hear."

Her heart started pounding. "Why? What did he say?"

"Albert Brenneman relayed to me that he and his wife do not want you to return to their home."

Mary was sure she'd heard wrong. "They don't want me to come back to Ohio? If they are worried about my health, I'm getting stronger every day. Once the doctor agrees, I'll be able to make the trip."

"That's not their reason."

"They don't want me?" She sank back against her chair in shock.

Glancing at Ash, she saw his gaze focused on the floor. She tried to make sense of what Bishop Schultz was saying. What reason could her in-laws have to abandon her? "It's not my fault that I have forgotten who they are. It's not deliberate. Can you make them understand?"

"They don't wish you to return because you have been shunned by your church."

Mary sprang to her feet. "That's not possible."

"Why do you say that?" the bishop asked gently.

"Because I know what that means. I would never break my vow to the church. What is it they say I have done?" Her gaze shot from Ash to his father, to Talitha standing behind her. "Tell me. What have I done?"

"Your father-in-law would not discuss it. I have written to your bishop asking for clarification. I await his answer."

The room was reeling. She sat down abruptly. "I don't understand. Ash, did you know about this?"

He looked at her then. She read pity in his eyes. "I did."

She pressed her hand to her chest. "Why didn't you tell me?"

"We hoped you would be able to explain when your memory returned," Talitha said.

Mary struggled to recall something that would explain this. "I don't know what I did. I have to repent to be accepted back into my church." She grew cold. A shiver shook her. She looked at Ash. "How can I repent if I don't know my sin?" she shouted.

Drawing a shaky breath, she strove for composure. "I'm sorry."

"You are understandably upset," the bishop said. "To continue your shunning when you have no memory of your offense does not seem right to me. To us. You have left your old church and arrived at a new one. We are all made new in Christ. He paid for our forgiveness with His blood. If it is your wish to join our community, then we welcome you. To become a member of our church requires that all our baptized members vote to accept you. That will happen in time if you are sincere in your desire to remain a member of the Amish faith and follow our Ordnung. I hope you can join us in worship tomorrow. It will be the best way for you to meet our people."

The bishop got to his feet and looked at Ash. "Your courtship may resume if that is still your wish. Knowing that may speed up her acceptance by everyone. I'll leave you to discuss it."

"What courtship?" Mary's gaze flew to Ash. "What is he talking about?"

"I can explain," Ash said calmly.

She got to her feet with her hand pressed to her pounding head. "You and I were courting? I don't understand. You said we'd never met?"

"It was all by mail."

"Why didn't you tell me that? What else haven't you told me?"

"There's no need to be upset," he said calmly.

"How can I not be upset? You deceived me." She rushed out the door leading to the garden. Outside, she glanced around, desperate for somewhere to hide, but there was nowhere.

"Mary, listen to me." Ash had followed her.

She turned to gape at him in shock. "Listen to you? Why should I listen to you? You knew all of this, and you never said a word. I thought I was going to get strong enough to go back to Ohio and my memory would return when I walked into my own house. Now I'm never going to do that. You shouldn't have given me hope. You shouldn't have kept secrets from me." Her voice broke. She pressed her lips together to stop their trembling.

"I'm sorry. We didn't know how to tell you about the shunning. It seemed cruel when you had no memory of what you had done."

"What would drive me to break my vows to

my church and turn my back on my family and friends? I need to know, Ash."

"Maybe it's for the best that you can't remember. You can make a new start here. Begin with a clean slate."

"A blank one, you mean." She tried to swallow the bitterness rising in her throat. God was asking too much of her. Anger at God and at Ash rolled into a stone in her stomach. "The bishop said we could continue our courtship. Is that why I'm here? Am I some kind of mail-order bride for you?"

"Don't be ridiculous."

"Am I wrong? Was marriage the reason I wanted to move to Maine?" Suddenly she realized what must have happened. "Oh, wait. I see now. I could never remarry back home. It would be forbidden to any Amish fellow to wed me. Who suggested I come here? Was it you or was it me?"

"You mentioned something about wanting to see the countryside and I invited you to visit."

The echoes of a conversation filled her mind. "My last chance for a family of my own." Had she heard them or spoken them?

"I'm sure that's not true," he said without conviction in his tone.

It had to be true. "Did we discuss marriage in our letters?"

"You were coming here to see if we would suit each other."

"But there was nothing definite between us." She could see in his face that there was more. "Tell me the truth, Ash. You've kept too many secrets from me. Tell me everything or I will never trust you again."

"I proposed in my last letter. You said you'd give me your answer when you arrived."

"Did I write to you about my shunning?"

"*Nee.*"

"So I lied by omission." Knowing she was capable of deception twisted a band of pain deep inside her mind. "I told your mother I was afraid I didn't want to remember because I might not like the person I was. Turns out that's true."

He stepped close and took her hand. "This has all been a shock. You would have told me everything."

"I won't marry you." She pulled away from him. "I can't marry you. We aren't courting. Not now. Not ever. I'm sure that comes as a great relief to you."

Ash gazed at her determined face and rubbed his hands on his pants. He cared for her more than he was willing to admit to anyone. He had to tread carefully.

He cleared his throat. "Actually, it is a relief.

I have regretted my proposal. It was an impulsive action and nothing good comes from decisions like that."

"Oh." Did she sound disappointed or insulted?

Holding up both hands, he added quickly, "Before I met you."

Anger flashed in her eyes. "Clearly after you met me, too, because you failed to mention it on any of the occasions that we were alone together."

This wasn't going the way he wanted it to. "Let's sit down and talk about this like reasonable adults."

She stamped her foot. "I don't want to be reasonable. I want to yell and scream at you."

"I understand. I'm sorry. I truly am." He turned away and crossed to a bench beneath a rose arbor.

She came over but sat as far away from him as she could get. "So talk."

"If you think about it rationally, you will realize why I couldn't tell you about our long-distance courtship."

"Engagement."

He tilted his head in denial. "You never gave me an answer, so we aren't technically engaged."

"You're splitting hairs. I came all this way."

"Okay, you're right. I decided not to mention our relationship because you were confused and frightened enough by your memory loss. I didn't want to add to your discomfort. What could I have said? Hi, you don't know me from Adam, but you're here to marry me. That's a little hard to work into a conversation."

"I guess I can see your point, but I did ask you why I wanted to come to Maine."

"And I told you part of the reason just not all of it."

"So you lied by omission."

"If that's the way you feel, then yes, I did, but I hope you can forgive me. I had your best interest at heart."

"I wish I could say the same about myself. My lie wasn't to protect anyone—it was to gain a new life. If only I could remember why."

"Mary, can you forgive me for not being completely truthful?"

She glared at him for a long moment, then the anger in her eyes faded. "Of course I forgive you, Ash. You have been my rock in a turbulent sea."

He smiled in relief.

"Where does this leave us?" she asked. "What do we do now?"

"I think we've become friends, haven't we?"

Her wry smile proved he had chosen the right words. She nodded. "We have."

"There's no reason we can't continue being friends."

She looked away. "I'm not the kind of person you should be friends with."

Was she right? He was troubled by her shunning. The bishop's decision to overlook it was the right one, but the fact remained that she had deliberately turned her back on her church for some reason.

Despite knowing that, he was drawn to her in a way that baffled him. He couldn't turn away from her.

He bent forward to see her face. "I met Mary Brenneman for the first time when you woke up in the hospital. That woman is the woman I'm friends with. You haven't done anything to change that."

A sad, lost look filled her eyes. "But before."

"This is after. It's where we start. Agreed?" He would do his best to support her.

"It's not like I have other options. No home, no family. No one wants me."

"You have us."

She stared at him for a long moment. He watched some inner struggle going on behind her eyes and wished he could help. Finally, she sighed and gave a hint of a smile. "I'm grateful. I couldn't ask for a better family. I don't have a brother, but if I did, I would want him to be as kind as you."

"Brothers are overrated. You and I are *goot* now, *ja*?"

"Ja."

"Then try to appear a little happier."

She rolled her eyes. "This is all I've got. Take it or leave it."

"Then I'll take it." He stood and held out his hand. "Come inside and have some breakfast."

"I don't think I'm hungry."

"That come in and watch me eat. I am starved."

"My life has been turned upside down and all you can think about is food."

"A man has to eat."

Her frown returned. "Will everyone in the community hear about this? Tomorrow is my first prayer service here. How will I face all those people?"

"The bishop and my family are the only ones who know the whole story, but others may find out. Secrets rarely remain secret in a tight-knit Amish community. You must be prepared to face the talk, but I'll stand by you."

She gazed up at him. "I believe you will. *Danki*."

"Of course. I'm your friend, remember? Let's go in."

The family, except for Moses, was gathered in the kitchen when Ash walked in with Mary. He noticed the card table was missing and realized the significance. His family accepted her as a member of the faithful. Gratitude overwhelmed him.

Ash squeezed her hand. Mary raised her chin. "Ash and I have agreed we are no longer courting."

He frowned. He wasn't expecting her to be so blunt.

"Oh, I'm sorry to hear that," his mother said. "I think the two of you are exactly right for each other."

Mary cast a startled glance his way. "I do care for Ash, but as a brother. He's been wonderfully supportive. Happily, we have put this courting nonsense behind us, and we're still friends. Right?" She punched his arm playfully.

"Right." He managed to keep his smile in place. Her feelings toward him were brotherly?

Chapter Six

Mary spent a restless night wondering how she could pretend she cared for Ash in a brotherly way. She was good at pretending, but not that good. It had been the only thing that had occurred to her when she heard his mother say they were right for each other.

She wasn't right for him. The bishop said they could continue the courtship, but she knew better. Now she understood why she had come to Maine in the first place.

She must have fostered a romantic relationship with Ash to flee the community that shunned her. Maybe she believed her shunning wouldn't become known in the far reaches of northern Maine. Ash deserved better than a woman with such a sly nature.

He might say it didn't matter, but it did. To her. What had she done? She needed to know.

From now on, she would treat Ash as a friend. Nothing more. For his sake and for her own. She knew how Ash thought. His overblown sense of guilt about the accident made him feel responsible for her. If he suspected her affections were deeper than friendship, that guilt might force him to press courtship again. It was up to her to convince him they should stay friends.

Denying her affection for him wouldn't work. They'd grown close in the days since her accident. Pretending otherwise would be impossible. Putting herself in a position where she could express some of her attachment to him was her best option.

It wasn't the perfect plan, but she couldn't give up her friendship with Ash. God had taken everything else from her. She needed Ash. To get through today and all the other days until her memory returned.

All she had to do was convince her heart to follow the plan.

The soft knock at her bedroom door told Mary she couldn't delay facing him any longer. "Come in."

Talitha opened the door. "We're almost ready to leave for church. Will you be joining us?"

Mary swallowed hard and nodded. She would be the oddity of the day. An object of speculation, covert glances, pity and outright curiosity. Ash had promised to stand beside her. She was counting on his strength to get through the ordeal.

Talitha came in and sat on the edge of the bed beside Mary. "You know you don't have to go."

"I'm physically able, and I have so much to be thankful for." She bit her lip and hoped Talitha would understand. "The real reason I'm going is selfish. I'm not sure that's the right frame of mind for worship."

Talitha smoothed a stray strand of hair from Mary's forehead and tucked it behind her ear. "You're going to have to explain."

"Every time I wake up, I have this feeling that what I'm searching for is right there. If I could just pull back the curtain and get a glimpse of my past, the rest would rush in to fill the void."

"I pray for that to happen."

"When I open my eyes, there's nothing. But maybe if I close my eyes while the congregation is praying and place my petition before *Gott* when we are gathered in His name, He will hear and answer my prayer. So I'm going because I want to be healed, and that is selfish. I should pray for His will to be done instead."

"I don't think you're selfish for wanting to be healed."

"You don't?"

"Nor do I believe *Gott* feels that way. We are all human. We pray for rain, for good crop prices, we pray our children will be healthy because we know *Gott* is a loving father who understands us and our frailties. Pray from your heart and know that He hears you. He will answer in His own time, not yours."

"I worry my faith isn't strong enough to endure the wait."

"I'm sure it is. What else is troubling you?"

"Everyone is going to stare." It seemed vain to say it out loud.

Talitha took Mary by the hand and helped her to her feet. "You won't be alone. Pamela, Esther and I will be beside you the whole time."

She couldn't stall any longer. "Then I reckon I'm ready."

Ash stood waiting for the women to come out by the family buggy. His brothers waited with him. He wasn't sure what to say to Mary after the events of yesterday. The one thing he was sure of was that he didn't see her as a sister. Her statement had shaken him.

Moses had been out doing chores when Ash and Mary made their announcement. "So the bishop gave you and Mary his blessing to continue your courtship. Her shunning in Ohio will be forgotten if she follows our Ordnung."

"That's right." Ash was happy for her. Whatever she had done would be forgotten, but he was still troubled. What had prompted such a serious step?

"But the courtship is off?" Moses looked puzzled.

Ash stared at his boots. "That's what she said."

"You sound disappointed. Are you?" Seth asked.

Was he? His feelings for Mary were still a jumble but being near her made him happy. "I'm not sure."

"What?" Gabe demanded. "Are you saying it could still happen?"

Ash shrugged. "You heard her. She thinks of me as a brother."

"Ouch." Moses shook his head. "That's a bad sign. A girl is over you for sure when she says one of two things. 'We can still be friends,' or 'I like you like a brother.' That's death to a romance."

"You aren't helping," Seth said between gritted teeth.

Moses aimed an annoyed glare his way. "I'm just being honest."

"He's right," Ash said. "I'm not the fellow who makes her heart race. I'm the guy who hid the truth and made a mess of things. She isn't what I expected, but I've come to like her. A lot. And not as a sister."

"Listen," Gabe said, casting a quick glance at

the front door. "You went about this courtship the wrong way, but there is still time to fix it."

Seth nodded. "If you don't want to end the relationship, you need to start at the beginning. Catch her interest."

Ash shook his head. "We already know each other. It's not like seeing a girl at a picnic for the first time and wondering if there could be something between you."

"It's exactly like that." Gabe grinned. "Forget everything you thought you knew about Mary and start courting her."

"What are you two talking about? How can I undo what's happened?"

Gabe and Seth put their hands on Ash's shoulders. "You can't undo it but think of it this way. Now you know she is a fine eligible woman according to our bishop. You're going to say something sweet to her. Do something nice for her. Then you gauge how she reacts just as you would with any woman."

Ash gave a grunt of disgust. "If I was any good at that kind of thing, I wouldn't have started a long-distance relationship by mail." What his brothers were suggesting would never work.

"I'll help," Moses said with a sly grin. "I can tell when a woman is interested. I'll let you know if you're on the right track."

Ash rolled his eyes at Moses. "You always

think the girl is interested in you. Remember when Waneta visited? You thought you had a romance going with Esther and Pamela's youngest sister, but once Nancy returned to Ohio, she got over you right quick."

"Moses has a point," Gabe said.

"I do?" Their little brother puffed up and grinned.

"It pains me to say it, but you do." Gabe turned to Ash. "We might be better at judging Mary's attitude toward you than you are. We can tell you what's working and what's not. Plus, Seth and I have wives who would be delighted with a bit of matchmaking. They can get the information you're after from the horse's mouth, so to speak."

Lifting his hat, Ash then raked his fingers through his hair and jammed his hat back on. "This is ridiculous. I don't want my family spying on Mary for me. I blew my chance with her. I have to accept that unless she tells me otherwise."

"Here they come. Say something nice to her," Moses muttered.

"You're being ridiculous," Ash said under his breath. He turned to smile at his father and the women coming down the porch steps.

"What have you got to lose?" Moses walked to the horses hitched in front of the family's largest buggy. It had three rows of seats and a storage box behind. Because it was a fine morning, they had rolled the door flaps up. They could be let down quickly if rain threatened. Moses wouldn't be riding with them. He was taking his courting buggy in case he had the chance to escort one of the single women home after the service.

Zeke helped his wife stow her baskets of food for the meal after the service. Esther and Pamela scrambled up into the center row of seats. Mary hesitated at the high step. Ash felt an elbow in his side.

He looked at Gabe, who nodded toward Mary. Maybe his brothers knew what they were talking about. He should at least explore the possibility.

Ash stepped forward. "Let me help."

She kept her gaze averted. "I'm not as agile as I used to be. At least I think I was nimbler."

He took her elbow to steady her as she stepped up. "Are your ribs paining you?"

"Only if I bend or stretch too far."

"Are you sure that you want to go to church?" He felt the nudge of another elbow and scowled at Seth behind him. Seth drew a grin on his face and smiled big.

"I'm glad you're coming," Ash said quickly. "I just hope it isn't too much for you."

He looked at Seth. His brother gave him two thumbs-up.

Mary took a seat beside Esther and looked

down at Ash. She wore a guarded expression, but then she relaxed. "You're sweet to be concerned. I'll be fine."

He felt another elbow. He was going to have a dozen bruises if his brothers kept this up. Seth wagged his eyebrows toward the front of the buggy where Moses mimicked driving.

Ash smiled at Mary. "I can bring you home if you get tired. Moses will let us borrow his rig. That way the others don't have to leave early."

He almost laughed at his little brother's pained expression.

Gabe, Seth and Ash took their places in the rear seat. Their father spoke to the team to get them moving. The bimonthly prayer service was being held at the home of Jesse and Gemma Crump on the other side of New Covenant. The ride would take forty minutes.

"Say something to her," Seth whispered in Ash's ear.

"Like what?" he whispered back.

"Something funny or fun."

Ash drew a blank. He shook his head. Seth gave an exasperated huff.

Ash racked his mind for something to say that wouldn't sound foolish. Why did he feel awkward with Mary now? He hadn't before. This was important to him. He didn't want to mess it up. A flash of red caught his eye between the trees.

He quickly tapped Mary's shoulder. "Look, your fox is watching us."

"Where?" She sat up eagerly.

"To the left by that gray boulder. See her?"

"Oh, I do. And there is her kit, too." She watched until they were past, then she turned in her seat to smile at Ash. "You were right. She didn't go far."

"She must have a den nearby."

"Do you think we could search for it? Not today, but maybe tomorrow?"

He thought of all he had to do. "I really should catch up on my work."

"Of course." She turned back around.

He got another elbow from Seth. Glaring at his brother, he cleared his throat. "If you give me a hand with the inventory in the morning, Mary, we could scout around in the afternoon."

She turned to him quickly and winced. "I have to remember I can't do that yet."

She didn't want to work with him. Doing inventory wasn't anyone's idea of fun. "Never mind. I can manage by myself."

"*Nee*, I'd love to help if I'll be of any use with one hand."

She liked to tease. He'd give it a try. "Do you remember how to count past ten?"

"Ash! That was mean." Pamela glared at him over the seat back, but Mary wore a huge grin.

Laying a finger against her cheek, she looked thoughtful. "I reckon I can get to twenty by taking off my shoes." She couldn't hold back a giggle.

The sparkle in her eyes made his heart light. "That'll work."

His feeling of awkwardness evaporated. Teasing a woman wasn't something he normally did, but with Mary it seemed natural.

The women faced forward again. Ash elbowed Seth in the ribs this time and shared a grin with his brothers. Gabe gave him two thumbs-up.

That hadn't been so bad. Mary congratulated herself for maintaining the right tone with Ash on the ride to the Crump farm. Lighthearted and cheerful. He had responded in kind. He'd even made a joke. She smiled again at the memory.

Pamela leaned toward her. "I'm glad to see you and Ash are getting along."

She signed her comment for Esther.

"He's a fine man. You could do worse," Esther added.

Mary's smile froze on her face. "We're friends."

"Of course." Pamela and Esther shared a speaking look, signed something to each other, grinned, but didn't explain.

Mary looked out the door. Friends teased each other, right? It didn't mean there was an attraction between them. She certainly didn't want Ash's family to think there was. It might be best to ignore him for the rest of the day. Then Pamela and Esther would see she wasn't enamored with him.

When they finally arrived at the home of Jesse and Gemma Crump, Zeke stopped the buggy in front of the house. Ash hopped out and offered his hand to Mary.

She held on to the carriage doorframe instead. "I can manage." Her tone was more abrupt than she had intended.

Nodding, he stepped aside, but she caught his puzzled expression. Had she hurt his feelings? This plan was turning out to be more difficult than she had imagined. She followed Pamela and Esther into the house.

The kitchen was a hub of activity as women set out food from various boxes and hampers while chatting and laughing. Mary stood back as Talitha bustled in with her baskets. She paused in the middle of the room. "May I have everyone's attention? Let me introduce Mary Brenneman from Ohio."

The room grew quiet as all eyes turned to her. Talitha put her basket down. "As I'm sure some of you have heard, she was in a terrible accident when a pickup truck struck her."

Murmurs of sympathy fluttered around the kitchen. Heat rose to Mary's cheeks.

"She has no memory of her life before waking up in the hospital. Not even her own name." Talitha paused.

The group remained quiet as they waited for her to continue. She took a step farther into the room. "The doctor called it traumatic amnesia. He believes her memory will return with time. She had been corresponding with my son Asher. We know she was coming to visit our community with the idea of moving here. We must pray for her recovery and do what we can to help her bear this burden as her new neighbors and friends."

A small red-haired woman with a sympathetic smile stepped forward. "*Wilkumm*, Mary. I'm Gemma Crump. This is my daughter Hope." She placed her hand on the head of the toddler at her side. "We're glad you could join us."

"*Danki.*" Mary returned the woman's smile.

"Let me introduce you to everyone else." Gemma led Mary around the room. She met the bishop's wife and a dozen other women, including Gemma's mother. Esther and Pamela stayed by her side the whole time. It was overwhelming, but not as uncomfortable as she had feared. Talitha's announcement had set the right tone and delivered all the pertinent information so Mary didn't have to retell the story.

A short time later, Mary followed the Fisher women as they moved down to a large open basement for the service.

The men had lined backless wooden benches up either side of the center aisle down the middle of the room. Men and boys would sit on one side while women and girls sat facing them on the other side. The bishop and ministers would take turns preaching in the middle between them. Married women sat in the front rows while the unmarried women and girls sat behind them. One elderly woman sat beside the benches in a wing-backed chair. It surprised Mary there weren't more elders. Maybe it was because New Covenant was a new congregation settled by younger families.

Bishop Schultz and two other men entered the room. Mary assumed they were the ministers. Behind them came the men. They removed their hats and hung them from rows of pegs on the back wall in a quiet and orderly fashion. Married men sat in front. The youngest boys took up the last row nearest the door to make a quick escape when the service ended. Ash and Moses sat behind their father and married brothers almost directly across from her. She refused to look at Ash, keeping her gaze lowered.

The Volsinger, the song leader, announced the first hymn. A wave of rustling ran through the room as people opened their copies of the *Ausbund*. Mary picked up the thick black songbook beside her. It contained the words of all the hymns the Amish used in their services. Composed by early martyrs of the faith during their persecution and imprisonment, the songs told of sorrow, despair, hope and God's promise of salvation. The melodies, passed down through generations, were learned by heart in childhood. Singing was done slowly and in unison without musical instruments. Mary joined in the beautiful chant-like opening hymn, delighted to find she remembered it.

How was it possible she could recall words to a song, but not who she was or where she came from?

During the hymn, Bishop Schultz and his two ministers went out to counsel in a separate room in the house where they would discuss the preaching for the day. None had prepared notes. Amish preachers spoke as God moved them. They stayed out for an hour while the rest of the church sang hymns. Despite her best intentions, Mary found her gaze wandering to where Ash sat. Several times she caught him looking at her. She immediately looked away.

When the bishop and preachers returned, the sermons started. The men spoke Deitsh or Pennsylvania Dutch, but the Bible readings were in

High German. After the readings, the men trans-
lated them into Deitsh so the young children
could understand. Amish children didn't learn
English and German until they started school.
Deitsh was the language spoken at home.

The sincerity of the sermons moved Mary. She
prayed earnestly with the congregation. She asked
the Lord to heal her and show her His will. The
hymns and prayers shared with the entire community filled Mary with a deep sense of peace,
but her memory didn't return as she had hoped.

The service lasted for three and a half hours.
During it she saw some of the youngest children
sit with one parent for a while and then get up to
sit with the other one. All the children were well-
behaved. Gemma had set up a small table where
the *kinder* took turns going to fill a baggy with
animal crackers if they became restless.

When the service concluded, she went outside
with Esther and Pamela while the men converted
the benches into tables for the meal. The men
would eat first and the women later. Esther and
Pamela stopped to talk to several of their friends.
Mary crossed to a small bench beneath an apple
tree and sat down. Her ribs and arm ached after
sitting up for so long. Her head started pounding, too.

Two young girls who looked about eight or

nine approached and stopped in front of her. "Do you really have ambezzia?" one asked.

"Amnesia," Mary said. "And *ja*, I do. Who are you?"

"I'm Maddie Gingrich. This is my friend Annabeth Beachy. My very best friend used to be Bubble, but she moved to Texas because she was imaginary. If you forget your homework, the teacher can't be mad at you because it isn't your fault. Is that true?"

"I guess it would be, but I don't go to school."

A speculative glint appeared in Maddie's eyes. "How can someone catch ambezzia?"

A slender woman with honey-brown hair and eyes as green as grass walked up to the pair and planted her hands on her hips. "It isn't catching, and you will not forget your homework again."

Maddie looked disappointed, but she nodded. "Okay."

"Told you it wouldn't work," Annabeth said. "Come on, let's go play."

The two girls ran off.

Mary chuckled, her headache momentarily forgotten. "That one is a handful, isn't she?"

"You have no idea. I'm Eva Gingrich. I'm married to Maddie's brother Willis. We are raising her and two of his younger brothers."

"From your tone I thought perhaps you were her teacher."

"I used to be, but my brother Danny has that unenviable task now. Sadly, Maddie has him wrapped around her little finger. I hope she didn't upset you with her questions."

"Not at all."

"It must be terribly distressing for you. I can't imagine."

Mary adjusted the sling that pulled at her shoulder and made it ache. "The doctor advised me against trying to force my memory to return, but that's impossible. The longer it goes on the more I lose hope."

"Perhaps you need something to take your mind off it. We're having a work frolic at the school this coming Thursday. Spring cleaning in the schoolhouse and the teacher's home next door. Why don't you come and help? I'm sure the children will entertain you."

It felt good to be included in a normal activity. Mary cocked her head to the side and gave a nod. "I believe I will. *Danki.*"

"Don't thank me yet. You haven't met my brother Danny. He's one hard taskmaster."

"I'm not worried after you told me Maddie has him wrapped around her finger."

Eva laughed. "I look forward to seeing you then."

As Eva walked away, Mary slumped and

rubbed her forehead. Why did she tire so easily? Why did her headaches keep coming back?

"You look about done in," Ash said, stepping around the side of the tree.

Her heart gave a happy skip at the sound of his voice. She should send him away, but she couldn't do it. "I love how you shower me with compliments."

He sat beside her. "You deserve every one. Are you ready to leave?"

"I want to stay. People are being kind. It hasn't been as hard as I imagined."

"Then stay."

"The truth is, I'm tired."

"And you have a headache."

"How did you know?"

He touched her forehead with his finger. "You're wearing your headache frown."

"I'm seldom without it, I'm afraid."

His dark brown eyes filled with concern. "Are they getting worse?"

"*Nee.* Mainly they come on when I'm tired."

"You need to rest more. I'll go get the buggy."

"I hate to take the buggy away from Moses. He might want to take a girl home after the singing tonight."

Ash got to his feet. "Moses will survive. I'm taking my girl home first."

She saw Pamela approaching. "I'm not your

girl, Ash," she said, loud enough for Pamela to hear.

"Right." Ash looked away, but not before she caught a flash of pain in his eyes. He walked off with his shoulders bent and his head down.

"What's wrong?" Pamela asked when she reached Mary's side.

"I have a headache. Ash is going to drive me home. Please tell everyone how much I enjoyed meeting them."

"I will. Is everything okay between you and Ash?"

"Sometimes he acts like we're still courting. I had to remind him we aren't. Tell Moses I'm sorry for taking his buggy."

"Don't worry about it. Give Ash some time to get over the relationship he thought he had with you. You don't remember any of it, but Ash had months to grow fond of the woman he was writing to and planning a future with."

"I'm sorry I wasn't honest with him then, but he needs to realize we're just friends now."

Pamela laid her hand on Mary's shoulder. "I understand."

Pamela walked away. Mary hoped she'd gotten her point across. She looked over to see Ash hitching Frisky to Moses's buggy.

"I can't be your girl, Ash. Not even if I want to be," she whispered.

Chapter Seven

Mary wasn't his girl. She had practically shouted it at him. Ash sat with his shoulders hunched against the sting as he drove toward home. He tried to ignore the pain, but he couldn't when she was sitting beside him. Why had he said that?

Because he wanted it to be true?

That was ridiculous. Completely ridiculous.

Mary remained withdrawn and silent as they headed home. She sat as far away from him on the buggy seat as she could get, looking lonely and dejected. The same way he felt. Was she still in pain?

"Are you okay?" he asked when they had been on the road for an uncomfortable two miles.

"I'm fine." Her curt reply wasn't encouraging.

"Is your headache worse?"

"*Nee*, it's fine." She stared off into the distance.

Ash pressed his lips together. He didn't need

his brothers to tell him Mary wasn't interested in conversing with him. He glanced at her sad face. A new thought hit him. He was feeling sorry for himself, but Mary was the important one. He needed to make this right between them.

"Are you still upset with me?" he asked.

That made her look at him. "Of course not."

He tipped his head in disagreement. "I think you are."

"What have I done that makes you say that?"

"It's not what you've done, it's just… Oh, never mind. I shouldn't have said anything."

She twisted in the seat to face him. "Tell me what you are about to say right this minute."

"Okay. This morning we were laughing together. I thought we were having a nice time. Then you almost took my head off for no reason. Now you can barely look at me."

She sighed and looked down. "I'm sorry, Ash. I didn't mean to hurt your feelings."

"Well, you did. I made a mistake when I said I'm going to take my girl home. I only meant I was going to take you home first."

"I understand that. Maybe I overreacted. It's difficult for me to know how to behave now. I enjoy your company, but I don't want people to assume we're courting when we aren't."

He was responsible for some of that. "By *peo-*

ple, do you mean my family? Because nobody else knows that we were except the bishop."

"Your mother, Pamela and Esther have all hinted that we make a *goot* couple. It puts me in an awkward position."

Another glance at her forlorn face made his heart tighten. He couldn't bear to be the cause of her unhappiness. He wanted to see her smile at him the way she used to. They shared something special. He wasn't willing to lose that.

"I'm sorry if my family made you uncomfortable, Mary."

"It isn't your fault. You're just being nice, the way you always are, but they see something else."

"Do you want me to stop being nice?"

She arched one eyebrow in disbelief. "Is that possible?"

He wanted to hear her laugh. "I could try. You look haggard today, Mary. More than usual. Have you forgotten anything new lately? Do you recall what color the sky is? Shall I give you a hint?"

She choked on a giggle, then sat up straight. "I might forget I'm not mad at you."

There was the smile he was after. "If I'm rude and you're angry, that should get the point across."

"I'm not sure you'll be convincing." She gave a deep sigh. "Maybe I should ask the bishop to take me in."

Ash's heart dropped. He didn't want her to move out of his home. "Don't do that. I'll talk to my family. I'll make it clear that you and I are just friends. How does that sound?"

"Really?"

"Of course. I'll set them straight. No more talk about leaving, okay?"

"I appreciate that. You *are* still my friend, Ash. You know that, don't you?"

"Sure." He wanted to be more than her friend, but that was a lost cause.

"Danki."

"For what?" He glanced at her, and his heart turned over at the sight of her sweet smile.

"For understanding. You are a remarkable fellow."

It was a bittersweet compliment. Why couldn't she see him as a potential mate rather than a friend? He stared straight ahead not wanting his feelings to show on his face. "The most exciting man you know, right?"

"Not anymore."

"What?" He looked at her in surprise. Did she like someone else? Who did she know?

"I think Moses is more exciting."

She was joking, wasn't she? "Moses? Exciting? I wouldn't say that."

"He owns this fine high-stepping mare and plush courting buggy. I wouldn't be surprised to learn that he's got a stereo in here." She opened the glove box. "Aha. Just as I thought."

She pulled out a portable radio with two large speakers. "I'm sorry, Ash. Your little brother is *much* more exciting than you are."

Ash swallowed what was left of his pride. "I'll let him know you think so."

"Please don't do that." She put the radio back. "I don't need anyone asking to walk out with me, especially your baby brother."

He gave her a puzzled look. "You don't?"

"Absolutely not."

"But you are free to see any of the single fellows in the community."

She grew somber. "I won't go out with anyone."

"I don't understand. Why not?"

"Because I'm incomplete." She looked away. "I can't be a part of someone's life until I have recovered my own."

What if that never happened? Would she live alone for the rest of her days? He grew sad at the thought. She had so much to offer. Surely that wasn't God's plan for her.

Ash wanted to reassure her, hold her close and tell her everything would be fine, but would it? He didn't have the right to do and say those things.

"Ash, stop!" Mary turned around in her seat.

"What? Why?" Ash drew back on the driving lines. Frisky came to a sliding standstill.

"I saw the little fox. It's hurt." She got down from the buggy.

"Mary, come back. An injured animal can be dangerous." She didn't heed him. He had no choice but to get out and follow her.

She stopped a dozen paces off the roadway and crouched down to peer under a fallen tree. "Oh, it has a broken leg. We have to help it."

The little red kit was huddled beneath the trunk, crying pitifully. Ash looked around. There was no sign of the mother or the other kit.

"We can't leave him here to suffer, Ash."

She was right. He knew what had to be done, although he hated the idea. "It will be kindest to put the poor thing out of its misery. I'll go home and get a gun."

She surged to her feet. "Asher Ethan Fisher, I will not allow such a thing!"

He'd never seen her so angry. "Mary, be reasonable. It's a wild animal."

"There must be something we can do. I know how much it is hurting, but bones will mend." Her voice broke.

"You can't take it home," he said as gently as he could. Surely she knew that.

Her chin quivered, but anger sparked in her

eyes. "You just watch me, Asher Ethan Fisher. I am going to save this animal."

"Mary, please."

She ignored him, knelt beside the log speaking softly to the young fox. "It's okay. I'm going to take care of you."

She inched closer. The fox growled and snapped at her. She jerked back.

Why couldn't she be reasonable? Ash took off his jacket. "Get back before it bites you. I know Moses keeps a horse blanket in the boot. Get it for me."

"What are you going to do?"

"I'm probably going to get bitten. Do as I say. We need something to wrap him in."

Mary rushed to the back of the buggy and opened the boot. She found the horse blanket along with a tightly woven rattan box with a top. Inside was an assortment of tools. She dumped the contents and was able to drag it one-handed to where Ash lay sprawled on the ground with his head under the log. She heard a lot of snarling from the animal before Ash emerged with the young fox bundled in his jacket.

She opened the lid for him. "I found this in the boot, too. Careful. We don't want to hurt him."

"Too bad he doesn't feel the same about me." He laid the struggling bundle in the hamper and slammed the lid shut. "Now that you have your fox in a box, what would you like to do?"

She chuckled. "Nice rhyme."

"Mary?" She heard the annoyance in his tone. "We need to take him to a veterinarian."

"That would be Doc Pike in Fort Craig, but it's Sunday. His office won't be open."

"Can we call his home from the phone shack?"

"We can. You must be prepared. He might say no to treating a wild fox."

"I understand. I won't let the poor little thing suffer longer than necessary."

"Okay. Get in."

After scrambling up into the buggy, she took the box when Ash handed it to her. *"Danki."*

"Don't thank me yet."

She looked down at him and smiled. "You were very brave."

He shook his head. *"Foolish* is the word I would use. I think you're rubbing off on me."

"We can't be practical all the time."

"I used to be. You're a bad influence." It didn't sound like he meant it, so she smiled. He walked around the back of the buggy and got in.

When they reached the phone shack near the Fisher farm, Ash got out to place the call while Mary held the hamper and talked softly to the little fox inside. "We're going to get you fixed up. It's going to be okay." She prayed she was telling the truth.

Ash came back after a few minutes. "Will he see us?" she asked.

"He's out on a call, but his wife told me where we can get help."

"Another vet?"

He shook his head. "There's a woman not far from here by the name of Walker. She takes in injured animals, nurses them and releases them back into the wild. I've never met her. She's something of a recluse."

"If she'll help, we have to ask."

"I agree."

Twenty minutes later, they turned off the highway where a crooked mailbox sat beside a large wooden crate with the word Donations crudely painted on it in white letters. They drove down a narrow, overgrown lane that stretched back into the forest. A small cottage came into view after a quarter of a mile.

The place had a neglected air about it. There were pickets missing in the fence that surrounded a tiny yard. The weathered siding needed painting, and the grass was overgrown. Across from the house were several large pens made of tightly woven wire. Some were covered with the same. Each held a large doghouse. A small deer lay curled up in one pen. Another held a bobcat watching the proceedings from the branches of a dead tree that had been placed inside the kennel. If the others had occupants, Mary couldn't see them.

A large mastiff lay in front of the cottage door. He gave a deep woof and sat up. The cottage door opened. A petite elderly woman stepped out. She wore blue jeans and a red flannel shirt. Her gray hair was pulled back in a long braid. She stood with her hands on her hips. "How can I help you?"

She didn't exactly sound welcoming.

"Are you Mrs. Walker?" he asked.

"I am."

"Mrs. Pike sent us. She thought you might be able to help." Ash stepped down from the buggy. He took the hamper from Mary, put it on the ground and then helped her out of the buggy.

"We found a little fox injured by the side of the road." Mary cautiously lifted the lid to peek inside.

Mrs. Walker came down the steps and crouched beside Mary. "How badly is it hurt?"

"It has a broken front leg. Can you help it?" Mary looked at the older woman's face. Up close, she could see Mrs. Walker had the most amazing deep violet eyes.

Suddenly Mary had a fleeting glimpse of a

man with eyes the same shape and color in his tan face. Lines of worry creased his brow.

The vision vanished. Mary shot to her feet as pain stabbed her temples. A roar grew in her ears. Mrs. Walker stared up at her with a quizzical expression. "Have we met before?"

Mary stumbled back a step and turned toward Ash. She reached for him as everything went dark.

Ash caught Mary as she crumpled. He swept her up in his arms. Her face was deathly pale. Panic hit him so hard he could barely breathe. "Mary? Can you hear me?"

Mrs. Walker stood and frowned at them. "I don't normally treat people but bring her inside." She hurried ahead to the door and pushed the big dog off to the side.

Ash followed her into a dim room with a faded blue sofa beneath a single window. She picked up a yellow tabby cat off the couch and deposited the animal in an armchair. Ash laid Mary gently on the cushions. He knelt beside her and held her hand. His heart hammered wildly with fear. She had to be okay.

"What's wrong with her?" Mrs. Walker asked.

"I don't know." Her face was so pale. "Should we call an ambulance? Do you have a phone?"

"I don't. Young man, look at me."

He tore his gaze away from Mary's still countenance and focused on the older woman.

She eyed him intently. "She has a cast on her arm and old bruises on her face. What happened to her?"

He sank back and rested on his heels. "She was hit by a pickup truck about a week and a half ago. She has a cracked rib, and she gets bad headaches. She has only been out of the hospital for a few days, but she wanted to attend church services today. I could tell she was in pain after the preaching. She agreed to go home early."

Mrs. Walker went to the sink in the tiny kitchen and wet a dish towel. "Okay. It sounds as if she is trying to do too much too quickly. Is she your wife?" She brought the damp cloth over and laid it on Mary's forehead, then grasped her wrist.

"*Nee*, but she is staying with my family. She also has amnesia."

"Her pulse is fine." She lifted each of Mary's eyelids. "Her pupils are equal. That's a good sign. She doesn't remember the accident. That's not uncommon."

"Mary doesn't remember anything from before the accident. She didn't even know her own name."

Mrs. Walker frowned. "That is concerning."

"You wondered if you had met her before. She's from Bounty, Ohio. Have you been there?"

She picked up a black bag from beside the sofa and pulled out a stethoscope. "I have not. Why don't you step out so I may examine her? You can put the young fox in one of the cages in the barn for me."

"All right." He got up reluctantly. He didn't want to leave Mary.

"She'll be fine. I'll call you if she needs anything."

He took one step away and hesitated. Mrs. Walker made shooing motions with her hand. "The sooner you go, the sooner you can come back. She'll be fine. I was a human nurse for many years until I discovered animals make better patients."

He nodded and walked out of the house. Standing on the porch, his feeling for Mary came into sharp focus. She was dear to him. Losing her would be unbearable.

The mastiff padded to his side and nuzzled his hand. He stroked the big dog's head. "You aren't much of a guard dog, are you?"

The dog sat beside Ash, wagging his tail.

Ash drew a shaky breath. How was he going to guard his heart now that Mary had found a way in?

She thought of him as a friend, someone as

close as a brother. He couldn't even be sure she was a suitable woman. Where did that leave him?

Nowhere.

He walked over, picked up the wicker box and carried it to a small barn. Inside, he found one large room with a dozen small cages lined up against the walls. Some of them had openings through the wall where the occupants could go outside. One cage held a sleeping opossum with a bandage around its side. Inside another cage was an owl. He couldn't see what was wrong with it. In various cubbies between the cages there were bottles, rolls of bandages, assorted instruments and towels.

After unlatching one of the vacant pens, he laid several towels on the floor of it, then positioned his box so the young fox only had one place to go. It took several minutes for the animal to decide to leave the safety of the hamper. When he finally did, Ash quickly latched the cage shut. The fox limped around the enclosure several times before settling in a corner on the towels.

"You're a lot of trouble. If it wasn't for you, Mary would be safe at home, and I wouldn't know how much she means to me. I'd still be content being her friend instead of being sick with worry for her and wondering what I'm going to do. Bringing you here might be the biggest mistake I've ever made."

He checked on Frisky and then went up to the house. He had to step over the dog to get in the door. He breathed a sigh of relief when he saw Mary sitting up on the sofa. Some color had returned to her cheeks, but she still looked wan.

She smiled when she saw him. "I can't believe I fainted. I'm sorry I frightened you."

He moved the cat to the floor and sat down on the chair opposite her. "How are you feeling?"

"Foolish."

"I'll have tea ready in a few minutes," Mrs. Walker said from the kitchen.

"That isn't necessary," Mary said. "We should be leaving."

Ash wasn't taking Mary anywhere until she was fully recovered. At the moment, she looked like she would topple over in a strong breeze. "Tea sounds wonderful, Mrs. Walker, *danki*."

"Please call me Naomi. Your friend is obstinate, Mr. Fisher."

"I don't like to be fussed over," Mary said.

Ash nodded. "*Ja*, Mary has a stubborn streak all right."

Mary lifted her chin. "I do not."

She was looking better by the minute. He relaxed and leaned back in his chair. "Who was it that insisted on crawling under a fallen tree to rescue a little fox when she was told she shouldn't?"

"I was merely concerned with the animal's welfare. And you were the one who crawled under the tree."

"Both you and that fox are *druvvel*."

Naomi laughed as she carried in two cups on a tray. "That will be a good name for him. Trouble."

Mary smiled at her. "You speak Deitsh?"

Naomi's grin faded. "I learned it as a child." Setting the cups down, she looked at Ash. "Make sure she drinks it all. I'm going to see if Trouble needs a cast. Sometimes in a young animal a leg break will heal without one if they can be kept quiet for a few weeks."

"We won't leave until she has finished her tea and is feeling up to the ride home."

"Good man." Naomi patted his shoulder and left the house.

Mary took a sip of her tea. Ash picked up his cup. "What happened, Mary?"

A faint frown creased her brow. "I'm not really sure. It was the strangest thing. Did you notice what bright violet eyes Naomi has?"

He shook his head. "I was too worried about you. You gave me quite a fright."

She blushed. "I am sorry. I didn't mean to."

"I know that. What about Naomi's eyes?"

"When I looked at her, I had a vision of a man with the same eyes."

"You saw a man with violet eyes?"

"It was more than the color. Their eyes were exactly the same. I don't know how to say it except if you look at Gabe's eyes they are exactly like Seth's."

"Identical."

She nodded. "I only saw it for a second before it faded. I tried to hold on to it, but then I had a sharp pain in my head. The next thing I knew, I was here on this couch. I think it was someone I know well."

He set his cup aside. "Then that is a good thing. Your memories are coming back."

Looking down, she shook her head. "I'd like to believe that, but the glimpses I've had are so few and vague that I have to wonder if I'm just imagining they are memories because I want them to be."

He slapped both hands on the tops of his thighs. "I say they are and that's that."

Rolling her eyes, she tipped her head toward him. "Not a rational conclusion, Ash. I disagree."

He liked the sparkle in her eyes when she teased him. "Finish your tea. If you're feeling well enough to argue, I think I can safely take you home."

"I'd like to visit Trouble first."

"Sure." He carried their cups into the kitchen and left them in the sink. When he came back, she was already on her feet. He eyed her closely. "Dizzy?"

"Not in the least."

"You will tell me if you start feeling poorly, *ja*?"

She stuck out her tongue. "You will stop coddling me, *ja*?"

He folded his arms over his chest. "Fine. Next time I'll let you hit the ground."

"*Nee*, you won't. You're too nice." She walked ahead of him out the door, patted the dog and then hurried toward the barn.

He stood on the porch and looked down at the dog. "*Druvvel*. That's the word for her. She's trouble for my peace of mind and maybe for my heart."

The mastiff wagged his tail and gave a short woof as if in agreement.

Mary entered the quiet barn and immediately saw Naomi standing by the small fox. The animal was stretched out on the table. She was listening to it with her stethoscope. When she took the instrument out of her ears, Mary took a step closer. "How is he?"

"Stable for now. I had to tranquilize him. He's going to need a cast. I don't think the bone is broken, but it may be cracked. I suspect he was hit by a car."

Mary gave her a wry smile. "That makes two of us."

"Your friend told me."

"Did he also tell you that I have amnesia?"

"He mentioned it."

"Before I fainted, I think you asked me if we had met before?"

Naomi began soaking a roll of plaster in a basin of water. "I thought you looked familiar, but your friend said you are from Ohio. I've never been there. I'm sorry."

"Don't be. This is the burden *Gott* has asked me to bear."

"I'm sure it's a trial for you, but it would be a blessing for some of us."

Mary frowned. "I don't understand."

Naomi began wrapping the bandage around the young fox's leg. "Some of us have a past we would like to forget, but the Lord decrees we must endure the memories of our mistakes."

"I'm sorry."

Naomi looked up from her task. "Don't be. We all receive gifts and challenges from our Father. It is how we use them and how we face them that matters."

Mary walked around looking into the cages. "You use your gift to ease the suffering of wild animals. I'm sure that must please Him. They are His creatures, after all."

She stopped in front of the owl. "What's wrong with this bird?"

"Someone found her with an arrow through her wing. It's illegal to hunt raptors but some people are cruel, and others are simply ignorant of the suffering they cause. She hasn't been eating. I'm worried about her. She doesn't seem to have the will to get better."

"Maybe she just needs more space. She can't see the sky in here. Do you have somewhere for her outside?" Mary looked at Naomi.

The woman was watching Mary with an odd expression on her face. "I've been meaning to build a small aviary, but I haven't finished it."

Mary smiled. "I know several young men that I can coerce into lending you a hand."

"I can manage. But thank you." Naomi turned her attention back to the fox. "I'm sure your friend is waiting for you."

Mary heard the dismissal in Naomi's voice. She had worn out her welcome. "Thank you for helping Trouble and all the other animals. May I come back and see him sometime?"

"Suit yourself." Naomi picked up the kit and returned him to his cage. "There you go. Sleep well, little one and never fear—"

"Only pleasant dreams are allowed in here," Mary finished.

Naomi turned to stare at her. "That's right. How did you know that?"

"I don't know. I must've heard it somewhere. Goodbye and thank you."

"Mary. Please do come again. You're welcome anytime."

Surprised at the warmth and sincerity of the sudden invitation, Mary nodded. "*Danki.* I'll do that."

Mary walked out to see Ash waiting in the buggy. She stepped up and sat beside him.

He turned Frisky toward the lane. Mary looked back and saw Naomi come out of the barn to watch them drive away. "There's something familiar about that woman."

"In what way?" he asked.

"This is the first time we've met, but it feels as if I've known her before. I wish I knew why."

Chapter Eight

Ash sent Mary up to rest as soon as they reached home. For once she didn't protest, and he was grateful. He put a pot of coffee on to perk and sat at the table waiting for his family to get home.

When they filed in the door, he had worked out what he wanted to say. "I need to speak to all of you. I made coffee." He signed as he spoke for Esther's benefit.

"What's going on?" his father asked.

"I need to clarify some things about Mary and me."

His family took their places around the table and waited for him to speak. No one bothered to get coffee. Ash cleared his throat. "Mary and I had a long talk on the way home. Gabe, Seth and Moses, earlier today you suggested I try courting Mary. That's not going to happen." They were hard words to speak, but they needed to be said.

His mother leaned forward in her chair. "Ash, the two of you seem so right for each other."

"Let him finish, Mamm," Pamela said, keeping her eyes lowered. She had to suspect what he was about to say.

Ash needed everyone to understand. "We know Mary has had a difficult time. I don't want to make things harder for her. The point is, she's not comfortable walking out with me. She doesn't feel that way about me. She likes me as a friend. There's never going to be more between us. She's made that clear."

He would do his best to keep his newfound feelings hidden. From his family and from Mary most of all.

"She may feel that way now, but things can change," Gabe said.

Ash gave his brother a sad smile. "I don't think that's going to happen. What I need from all of you is to accept that Mary's feelings for me are not romantic. Don't hint that we belong together or try getting her to change her mind."

He looked directly at his mother. "Or scheme to put us together. I know you have the best intentions. I love you for it, but please don't. It makes her uncomfortable."

"What about your feelings?" his mother asked.

"Mary's happiness is important to me. I want her to feel welcome in our home for as long as she wishes to stay. She likes all of us and doesn't want to hurt anyone's feelings."

"We like her," Esther said.

"But we don't want to see you miserable," Seth said.

"You deserve happiness, too," Gabe insisted.

Ash loved his brothers more than ever at that moment. "Am I disappointed that Mary isn't attracted to me? I am. What man wouldn't be. I had an idea of how I expected my life to go. I wanted the same kind of relationship I see Gabe and Seth have with Esther and Pamela. I thought I was ready to start my own family. I didn't want to feel left out. Someday those things will happen for me if *Gott* wills it. Just not with Mary. For now, I'm going to concentrate on helping her recover. I appreciate you hearing me out."

"You can't turn off your affections at will," Ash's mother said. "Trying to do so can lead to bitterness."

He shrugged. "I'm not denying how I feel about Mary. I like her tremendously. She's funny and unexpected. She's a sweet person and I treasure her friendship."

His mother's eyes narrowed. "It isn't that simple."

Ash's father rose to his feet. "Talitha, the boy has had his say. Leave him be. We will respect your feelings and those of Mary."

"Thanks, *Daed*."

His father nodded. "Come on, boys. The evening chores won't do themselves." He went to change out of his Sunday clothes. Everyone else did the same except for Ash's mother who stayed at the table.

Ash walked over and put his arm around her shoulders. "I'm okay. Don't worry about me."

"To worry is to doubt *Gott's* goodness and mercy. To fret a little for her children is a mother's duty."

"Well, please don't fret over me, then."

She reached up and cupped his cheek. "You might as well ask me not to breathe. I like Mary. She's teaching you to enjoy yourself. I've seen the two of you smiling and laughing with each other."

"That's what friends do."

"I reckon you must find your own way. Perhaps I'll write to Cousin Waneta and see if she has any advice."

Ash had to smile. "Save your matchmaking for Moses. Did you know he has a radio in his buggy?"

"Of course. I knew you boys had one in the barn during your *rumspringa*. Your father had one in his buggy when we were courting. We even danced a few times to the music when we were alone."

"Mother! I'm shocked."

She nudged him with her shoulder. "I wasn't born old, you know."

Ash laughed and hugged her again. "You aren't old. You are ageless."

"I enjoy a little flattery, but now it's time for you to get out of my kitchen. I must start on supper. Be assured that we will all help you take care of Mary."

"I know that." He started to leave the room then stopped on the threshold. "What do you know about Naomi Walker?"

"The woman who takes in animals?"

"That's the one."

"Not much. She came from Maryland about a year ago. I heard her husband walked out on her, but I don't know that for sure. I visited her once, but she isn't fond of company. She prefers her animals. Why do you ask?"

"Mary and I found an injured fox on the way home. We took it to her. Did she used to be Amish?"

"I've not heard that. I know she worked as a nurse and a missionary in Africa. If she was Amish once, she is *Englisch* now."

"Mary feels that she may have met Naomi before, but Naomi claims she didn't recognize her."

"Is that so strange? We all meet people who look familiar but aren't."

"Maybe you're right. It upset Mary."

"I pray her memory comes back soon. It's so hard on the child."

"I'd better get changed and help with the chores. Was Moses upset that we borrowed his girl-magnet?"

"His fancy horse and buggy? *Nee.* He spent the rest of the afternoon basking in the praise of several young women who mentioned how generous and unselfish he was."

Ash laughed. "Of course he turned it to his advantage. I pity the woman who falls for him."

His mother grinned. "She'll have her work cut out for her, for sure."

Mary joined the family for supper after a refreshing nap. Amish meals were for eating, not talking so it was a quiet affair. After supper, the family gathered in the large living room, as was their custom in the evenings. The French doors were opened. The breeze carried in the scent of roses and the sound of chirping birds gathering around the feeders throughout the garden. The evening light slowly faded. Ash went around lighting the lamps before he sat down with a book.

Zeke and Talitha were in their wing-backed chairs with the lamp table between them. Zeke read aloud from the Bible while Talitha relaxed with her knitting. Gabe challenged Seth to a game of checkers. Esther and Pamela got out a board game and invited Mary and Moses to join them. It was a game Mary knew. She was soon winning over protests from Moses.

When she looked up, she found Ash watching her. She wasn't sure if the soft light in his eyes was due to the lantern glow or some deep emotion. He smiled and her heart soared, only to plummet a second later. She wasn't his girl and never could be. No matter how much she wanted a life like this with him.

Talitha laid her knitting in her lap. "Ash told us you had an adventure after you left church, Mary."

She put away her sad thoughts and smiled. "We did, but Ash should tell it."

"Mary wanted to bring home a baby fox with a broken leg," he said.

"Where is it?" Pamela asked.

"We took it to Mrs. Walker," Mary said. "After Ash bravely crawled under a fallen tree to rescue it."

"This is a story we need to hear." Gabe turned in his chair to face Ash.

Mary and Ash recounted their experience with the injured fox. Gabe and Moses immediately started teasing Ash about being a fox terrier digging after his furry prize. Ash tolerated it with good humor. Mary had to add what she thought of his bravery. She didn't mention her fainting spell. Neither did he. She was thankful for that.

The many glances she intercepted between the family members led her to suspect Ash had already spoken to them about her concerns. Later, she took on Seth in a game of checkers and won. His defeated moan had everyone laughing. She glanced at Ash. He grinned and nodded encouragingly. She relaxed. It felt wonderful to be included in their warm family group. It was the best night she'd had since leaving the hospital. If only it could go on forever.

Early the next morning, she went out to the workshop to see if she could earn her keep by helping with his inventory.

Zeke and Seth were putting a red-hot metal rim on a wooden wheel outside the barn. Steam hissed and sputtered as they cooled it in a water trough. Moses was tacking black vinyl upholstery to a new buggy seat.

Ash was in the small office area with a large ledger open on the counter and a pencil tucked behind his ear. She knocked on the doorjamb. "Am I interrupting you?"

"Not at all. Have a seat." He indicated a high stool beside him. After pulling the pencil from behind his ear, he jotted several numbers on a scrap of paper. "Something isn't right."

"What's the problem?"

"The parts count is off. We should have five more wheel hubs. I'll need to order more if we don't, but they're expensive. I can't account for them."

"Have you asked the others?"

"I was getting ready to do that." He laid the pencil down. "What's up with you? How are you feeling today? You look less haggard. Have you forgotten anything new?"

"You are not being nice."

"I thought that's what we agreed on? Me not being nice. You being angry with me."

"That was plan A. Plan B was for you to talk to your family. I take it you did."

He nodded. "Everyone accepts that we'll remain friends. No one will suggest otherwise."

"Goot." She blew out a breath. There wouldn't be external pressure on her now, but she still had to deal with her own longings. He was such a wonderful man. Any woman would be blessed to have Ash walk out with her. Except the one who had schemed to gain his affection.

She smiled brightly to hide her somber thoughts. "How can I help today?"

"Find five wheel hubs."

"Okay? Where are your parts kept?"

"I'll show you. We have a separate storeroom at the back." He led the way past the glowing forge to another room filled from floor to ceiling with shelves and bins overflowing with bits and pieces of metal, wood and numerous bolts of fabric.

She could see organization wasn't a high priority for the Fisher men. "How can you find anything?"

"I have suggested we use a better system. I even labeled the drawers alphabetically, but it didn't help. This is just what everyone is used to. They claim they can't find anything when I put stuff away."

"Okay, am I searching for metal or wooden hubs?"

"Short metal. You look for them and I'll start counting the bolts and nuts. That takes the most time."

After searching through a dozen boxes, Mary located the missing hubs in an unmarked bin behind the door. "Found them!"

"How many?" He opened his ledger to the correct page.

"Four."

"Are you sure?"

"I didn't even need to take my shoes off to count that high."

He chuckled. "Fine. We're still missing one."

"One what?" Zeke asked from the doorway.

"One short metal wheel hub."

"Oh. I sold one to Willis Gingrich last week."

Ash pressed his lips into a tight line. "It's not written down."

"I was getting around to it." Zeke grinned at Mary. "Has he put you to work, too?"

"Just until the inventory is complete."

"I don't mind you taking over that task. Ash, Seth needs a leaf spring and a helper spring."

"Okay, I'll get them." Ash handed Mary his ledger. "Finish counting the six-inch bolts. I'll be right back."

She took the book from him and held it against her chest. "I know I said I wanted to look for the vixen's den this afternoon, but could we go back to Naomi's place instead?"

"Are you concerned about Trouble?"

She was more interested in talking to Naomi, but Trouble provided her a good excuse to visit. "I'm sure he's fine, but I would like to check on him."

Ash nodded. "Okay. I'll drive you over after lunch."

"If we're done with this." She patted the ledger.

"Even if we don't get finished, I'll drive you. The parts will still be here tomorrow. Unless Daed sells some while I'm not looking."

She grinned. "Take those springs to Seth. I can count faster if you aren't here."

"It's better to be accurate than fast," he cautioned as he went out the door.

Mary glanced at the book she was holding against her chest. She would do the best job possible because it was important to him. She eyed the floor-to-ceiling stack of bins. "Six-inch bolts, where are you?"

They finished the inventory by one o'clock. After a late lunch of cold cuts and lemonade, Mary eagerly climbed into the buggy next to Ash. "I'm sorry you have to drive me, but I don't think I can handle the lines with one hand."

"I'm eager to see how Trouble is faring, too. Are you sure you aren't too tired?"

"Not a bit. How am I going to pay for Trouble's care? I don't have any money."

"According to your letters, you do. You have a substantial amount in the bank from the sale of your husband's business."

Her mouth dropped open. "I have money?"

"That's what you wrote."

"What a relief. I don't know why I assumed I was poor. What type of business did my husband have?"

"I don't know. You never said."

"How can I get some of my money? Don't I need a checkbook or something?"

"The next time we go into Presque Isle, I will take you to our bank. Maybe they can arrange for a transfer of funds. It might be difficult without your ID and Social Security card. I reckon the police would have told us if they had recovered you purse."

She cocked her head slightly. "I wonder why I sold the business. Why didn't I continue to run it? Or hire someone to run it. Managing a business would be easier than being a farmhand for my father-in-law, don't you think?"

"That would depend on the business."

"You're right. This is so exciting. I have money! Are you sure I have a lot of money?" She saw he was trying not to laugh at her.

"Substantial was the word you used."

She tried not to get her hopes up. "That could be twenty dollars."

"I'm pretty sure 'substantial' is more than twenty dollars, but I wouldn't start spending it until you know for sure you can get it."

"Of course not. I was thinking I could pay something on my medical bills." She turned in the seat to stare at him as a troubling thought occurred to her. "My old church won't take up a collection for me, will they?"

He shook his head. "I made other arrangements."

A sick feeling settled in her stomach. "You are paying my bills. Oh, Ash, I can't let you do that. It must be thousands of dollars."

"The hospital will work with you. Bishop Schultz can make a general appeal for assistance since he isn't supporting your shunning."

She sat back and rubbed her shoulder. "I'll repay you when I can. Which may not be soon. Well, it was fun having a 'substantial' amount of money for a bit. I think I'm used to being low on funds, anyway."

Sadness lowered her spirits as she wondered about the husband she couldn't remember. He must have been the love of her life. She glanced at Ash. When her memory came back, would she see him in a different light? Would her attraction to him pale against the love she'd had for Edmond Brenneman?

"Somehow it doesn't seem right to use the money when I don't remember the man who earned it. It was his business, his hard work."

Ash gave her a funny look. "You were his wife. I'm sure you helped."

"I hope so. I'd rather leave his funds alone for now and find a job. Start supporting myself instead of living off the charity of your family. I wonder what I can do?"

"Mary, I'm sure you can do whatever you put your mind to."

She smiled her thanks for his confidence. "Maybe someone local needs an experienced farmhand who can handle a team of four draft horses."

"It might be practical to wait until you get your cast off before you apply for that type of job."

Flexing her fingers, she gritted her teeth at the discomfort. They were still stiff. Her forearm ached when she moved them. "There you go being practical again, but in this case, I reckon you're right."

Dejected by the thought of waiting weeks yet before she could seek work, Mary fell silent.

It wasn't long before Ash turned off the highway at Mrs. Walker's lane. When they came out of the trees, Mary saw Naomi nailing a roll of chicken wire to a tall post.

She saw them and walked toward the buggy with her hammer in hand. "I wasn't expecting to see you so soon. Have you brought me another patient?"

Mary gazed at her face for some spark of recognition. Naomi's welcoming expression turned puzzled. "What is it?"

Mary sighed in disappointment. "Yesterday I thought I recognized you, or rather someone who looks like you. I was hoping that seeing you again would bring back that memory."

"I see by your face that it hasn't."

"*Nee*. That's always the way. I have flashes

that I think are memories, but they never expand into something that I can be sure is real."

"You poor child. How terribly difficult that must be for you. But you have come to see Trouble, too, I'm sure."

Mary smiled. "I have. How is he?"

"Hopping about a little. He's not happy with the cone I had to put around his neck to keep him from chewing his cast but otherwise he's doing well. I saw his mother hanging out beside the barn last night. She must've followed you here. I plan to move him to an outside pen so they can be near each other. I hope she doesn't abandon him. He'll need her when he's well and can be released. He's too young to manage alone."

Ash came to stand beside Mary. "Are you building him a bigger pen?"

Naomi looked over her shoulder. "That will be an aviary. I picked up enough wire to finish it yesterday."

"Is it for the little owl?" Mary asked.

"I got to thinking about what you said, and you might be right. She needs more space to stretch out her wings. Would you like some tea?"

"I don't want to take you away from your work," Mary said.

Ash held out his hand. "I can finish nailing up the wire if the two of you would like to visit for a while."

Naomi handed over the hammer. "I knew I liked you."

She tipped her head toward the barn. "Come see your Trouble first."

Mary and Ash followed her into the barn where the young fox was sitting up in his kennel looking a bit ridiculous with the white plastic cone around his neck and a cast on one leg.

Mary walked up to the cage, delighted to see the baby looking so bright-eyed. "Hello, beautiful *bobbli*. I know it's awkward and uncomfortable, but in a few days, it will start feeling better. Then it will start to itch. I hope Naomi has something to help with that."

"He's growing fast so I'll have to change the cast in a week. I'll make sure to give him a good scratch while it's off."

The kit limped forward to sniff and then lick Mary's fingers. She looked at Ash. "Aren't you glad you rescued him now instead of the alternative?"

"You don't know how glad I am that I didn't have to choose the alternative." His relief was written on his face.

"Come up to the house when you're finished with the aviary, Ash," Naomi said. "I made fresh blueberry scones this morning. I love them but I don't need to eat them all by myself."

"Sounds *goot*."

Mary watched as he went out the door. The room seemed emptier without him.

"You have yourself a nice young man," Naomi said.

Mary turned to correct Naomi's assumption. "It's not like that. He is not my young man. He's a friend. That's all."

Naomi arched one eyebrow. "Funny, that's not the impression I get from the two of you."

"You're seeing something that isn't there." Mary couldn't look at Naomi. Was her attraction to Ash so strong that even a stranger could see it?

"Now you aren't being truthful."

Mary sighed deeply. "There can't be anything between us no matter how I feel about him."

"Is he married? Are you?"

"Neither one of us is."

"Then what's the problem?"

Mary stared into Naomi's sympathetic and somehow familiar eyes. A feeling that she could trust this woman filled her. She desperately needed someone to confide in. "It's so complicated."

"Aha. Then this conversation definitely calls for tea." Naomi marched out of the barn. Mary followed her up to the house.

Naomi pointed to the table. "Have a seat."

"Is there something I can do to help?"

"There's butter for the scones in the fridge. You can set that out. Some cups and plates, too."

When the table was set, Naomi brought a white china teapot decorated with pink roses there, filled the cups and sat down. She folded her hands. "Now, what seems to be the trouble between you and Ash?"

"Everything."

Naomi broke off a piece of scone. "This may call for two cups of tea. Try to be more specific."

Where did she start? Mary bowed her head. "I recently learned that Ash and I have corresponded for months before I came here. The relationship became romantic in nature. He proposed marriage."

"Before you met each other?"

"Apparently, I was coming to New Covenant to give him my answer. Why would I come all this way to tell him no?"

"Good point. You don't remember any of this?"

"Nothing."

"That must be disconcerting, but I'm still confused. You've met now. I can tell you like him a lot. Where's the problem?"

"I also learned I am shunned by my church in Ohio."

"Oh dear. I know what that means for an Amish person. I'm sorry."

"The thing is, I didn't tell Ash about my shunning in any of my letters. I was coming here under false pretenses. Maybe my letters were just a trick so I could start over in a new place."

"Seems a bit drastic. You don't strike me as the conniving sort."

"How can you say that? You barely know me."

"In my experience, which is vast compared to yours, child, conniving women rarely go out of their way to rescue an injured baby fox."

"But what if I'm not a good person? Don't you see? I can't allow myself to fall for Ash until I'm sure. Until my memory returns and I know what my feelings for him were, and why I tried to hide my shunning."

"*Were* is the key word in your argument. Aren't your current emotions more important than what you thought months ago?"

"I need to know, Naomi. I can't build a life with anyone until I know who I am."

"And if your memory doesn't return?"

"Then I'll have to go back to Ohio and learn what I can from the people who knew me."

"The people who shunned you. What if they won't speak to you? You know that's possible."

"I'll have to face that if it comes." Mary took a sip of her tea. It was lukewarm.

Naomi took a sip and put her cup down. "This is just my opinion, but I believe it is more important to be the best person that you can be now rather than worry about the past. I've made some heartbreaking choices in my life. I hurt the people I loved most. I lost the respect of my only son. We never spoke again and now he's gone so we never will."

Naomi reached across the table and laid her hand over Mary's. "But nothing in the past can be changed. When you accept that with your whole heart then you can begin to live as you should."

Was Naomi right? Could she let go of a past she couldn't remember? Or would it come roaring back and destroy her future?

Chapter Nine

Mary drew a shaky breath. She couldn't follow Naomi's advice. Knowing something from her past could hurt Ash made it impossible to reveal her feelings for him. Wouldn't it be less painful for him to lose a friend than the woman who cared so much for him?

"*Danki*, Naomi. I appreciate your concern."

"*Du bischt wilkumm.*"

"Your Deitsh is pretty *goot*."

Naomi looked toward the door. "Ash is taking a long time to finish that pen."

Movement caught Mary's eye. She turned to see a half-grown yellow tabby with white socks come staggering into the kitchen. The kitten came up to her, sniffed her ankle, then started purring and rubbing against her leg while struggling to stay upright.

"You poor little thing, what's wrong with you?" Mary picked her up.

"That's Weeble. Someone dropped her in my donation box. It was fortunate that I heard her cries when I went to collect the mail. She has CH. Cerebellar hypoplasia. More commonly called wobbly kitten syndrome."

"Will she get better?" Mary rubbed the kitten under the chin. A white bib that came up to her cheeks looked as if someone had glued cotton balls beside her nose. Weeble sat up and tried to bat the ribbons of Mary's *kapp*.

"She was born like this," Naomi said. "She may gain a little more muscle control, but she'll never get better. She's usually very shy and wary of strangers. I'm surprised she came out to meet you."

"I'm certainly glad you did, Wobbly Weeble. You're adorable."

Naomi looked at Mary intently. "Don't you feel sorry for her?"

The kitten had snagged Mary's ribbon and was trying to pull it to her mouth, but her head bobbed too much to bite it. Mary laughed. "Why should I? She doesn't know there's anything wrong with her. She just wants to play."

"Not everyone feels that way. I'm glad you do. Let's find out what's keeping Ash."

Mary put the kitten down and followed Naomi

outside. The aviary was finished, but she didn't see Ash. The sound of hammering started behind the barn. The two women walked in that direction.

When they rounded the back corner of the building, Mary saw Ash fitting a top to a wooden box and nailing it in place. He looked up and smiled at her. "Did I miss the scones?"

"We saved you some. What are you doing?" Mary studied his project.

Naomi's face brightened with delight. "He's made an owl box."

He held it up. The rectangular box had a perch and a hole in the front. "I thought your feathered guest might like some privacy. My brother Gabe is an avid birdwatcher. We've got a few of these around the farm among other birdhouses."

"It's wonderful. Thank you, Ash. If you'll put it up, I'll get Bundi."

He chuckled. "You named your owl Bundi?"

She grinned. "It's a Swahili word. It means owl. So original. Mary, would you like to move Bundi to her new home?"

"Of course I would." She grinned at Ash. His smile widened, and Mary's heart beat faster. She was falling hard for Asher Ethan Fisher. That wasn't what she wanted.

But maybe Naomi was right, and it didn't matter what Mary had thought of him in the past or how she had acted. Could she accept that and live in the here and now? Could they be more than friends?

"What?" he asked, and she realized she had been staring at him.

What if they grew close and then something from the past hurt him or changed his feelings for her? She couldn't bear that. "Nothing."

"The owl?" Naomi prompted from the barn's doorway.

"Coming." Mary hurried to the door.

Inside, Naomi handed Mary a large pair of gloves. "Put on these gauntlets. They'll protect you from her talons."

Mary slipped her arm out of her sling. The large leather glove fit over her cast. She pulled on the other one. "I'm ready."

"Move slowly. Allow her to step onto your hand—don't grab her."

Mary did as Naomi told her and soon had a grip on the owl's feet. Holding her gently, she lifted her out of the cage and carried her outside to the new enclosure, speaking softly to ease the bird's anxiety. Bundi stayed calm. Ash had secured the box to the trunk of a dead tree inside the pen. Mary settled the owl on a branch next to the perch and stepped away.

Bundi looked all around, stretched out her wings and then scurried up the branch to the box.

She checked it over carefully and then climbed inside. A second later she poked her head out the hole as if to say she approved.

"She looks happy." Mary prayed the little owl would feel at home under the starry sky tonight and grow confident again.

"You did well," Ash said.

Naomi nodded. "She has a gift. Animals seem to trust her."

Mary giggled. "A gift for handling owls. I wonder how I can translate that into a paying job?"

Naomi tipped her head. "Are you looking for work?"

"I haven't started, but I should. I've been living on charity for too long."

Naomi looked Mary up and down. "I know a crabby recluse who needs a part-time helper at her animal sanctuary. The pay isn't much, but you can set your own hours."

"You'd hire me?"

"On a two-week trial basis."

Mary couldn't believe her good fortune. "I accept."

"The animals will need to be fed and watered. Some need medication, and that isn't always easy. You'll have to clean the cages and take care of new arrivals."

"I can do it. I may not be fast because of my arm, but I'll do a good job for you."

"Well, I'm willing to try it if you are."

Mary's excitement ebbed away. "I don't have transportation to get here and back."

"I can bring you in the mornings if Mrs. Walker can see that you get home," Ash said.

"My pickup is temperamental, but I'm sure it can make a short trip. When can you start?"

Mary looked at Ash. "The school frolic is Thursday. Why don't I come Friday and Saturday?"

"That's fine with me," he said.

Naomi nodded and smiled. "That works for me. Ash, I promised you tea and scones. Come on inside."

"You can meet Naomi's kitten. Her name is Weeble, and she is adorable. I might have to sneak her home with us."

Ash's eyes widened. "You're allergic to cats, Mary."

"I am?" That was a surprise.

"You wrote that your mother-in-law brought a cat into the house. You broke out in hives, yet she refused to get rid of the animal."

Naomi's eyes darkened with concern. "She was holding the kitten a few minutes ago. If it was a severe allergy, she would've had a reaction by now."

"I feel fine." Mary checked her hand and arm. "No itching, no red bumps."

Naomi put her fingers on Mary's wrist. "Any tightness in your throat or chest?"

"Nee." She took a deep breath to prove it.

Naomi released her hand. "Your pulse is fine."

Ash didn't look convinced. "You were a nurse. Can someone get over an allergy?"

"It occasionally happens. Some children outgrow their sensitivity."

Mary chuckled and nudged Ash. "Maybe my mother-in-law gave me hives, and I just thought it was her cat."

Both Naomi and Ash scowled at her levity.

"Monitor her for the next hour or so to see if she develops symptoms. Best not to expose her to the kitten again until we're sure she doesn't have a delayed reaction. I will see you on Friday, Mary. Be ready to work."

Mary impulsively hugged the woman. "I can't thank you enough."

"Just do your job. That will be thanks enough." She turned and walked into the house.

Mary grinned at Ash. "She tries to be gruff, but she isn't. Not really."

"Are you sure you feel okay? Can I get you some water?"

"Ash, you're doing that thing I don't like."

"Showing concern?" he snapped.

"Fussing. Will you stop!"

His frown deepened. "*Nee*, because you need someone to look after you."

She glanced at the house and then tried to sound calm. "I don't want Naomi to see us quarreling. Let's just go home."

He kept quiet until they were back on the highway. "Did you sense you know Naomi from somewhere today?"

At least he wasn't asking her how she felt again. That seemed to be the main theme of their relationship. "I may have imagined that. I didn't have any kind of reaction when I saw her this time."

"The two of you seem to get along well."

"I know. I am glad she offered me a job. I'm employed. Isn't that great?"

"I'm not sure I've ever seen someone so happy to be cleaning out animal pens."

She wrinkled her nose at him. "You would point out the downside."

"I'm just being practical. I've got some rubber boots and gloves you can borrow."

"You can't burst my bubble. I'm going to love working with the animals and with Naomi. So there." She stuck her tongue out at him like he was a childhood friend.

That wasn't how she saw him, but she couldn't let him learn her true feelings.

* * *

Ash had never been so tempted to kiss a woman. Mary was impertinent and impractical. She annoyed him, and she was utterly adorable.

And that was not how he should be thinking about a sister or a friend. He concentrated on driving.

"I definitely want to repaint her donation box. I think she needs a sign by the highway telling people about her sanctuary. I'm sure not everyone knows where they can take an injured wild animal or injured bird."

"The vet sends people like us to her."

"True, but folks might be more inclined to help a wild animal if they know they won't have to pay a veterinarian to see it."

"You should discuss your plans with Naomi first. She might not want more creatures. It costs money to take care of them."

"That's a good point. Perhaps we can have a fundraiser for her. I'm sure your mother will have a few ideas. I can't wait to discuss it with her."

That evening Ash sat in the corner with his book in his lap and watched Mary with his family. She and his mother had their heads together for a while discussing money-raising projects for the sanctuary. After that, Esther began teaching her the sign alphabet from a picture book.

Mary had no trouble laughing at herself when she made a mistake.

Not serious, not practical, just charming. How could he have been so wrong about her? He wished he'd kept her letters. Now that he knew her, he wanted to reread them and see if he'd come to the wrong conclusion, because that's what he thought he wanted in a relationship.

Gabe came over to sit on the arm of Esther's chair. *You should ask her to spell our announcement*, he signed.

Esther grinned and looked at Mary. "What does this spell?" Her fingers moved rapidly.

"Wait. Slow down."

Esther and Gabe grinned at each other. "Say the letters out loud," Gabe suggested. "It will help you visualize the word."

Esther signed the first letter.

"*B*. Is that right?" Mary looked to Esther for confirmation.

Esther nodded and signed the second letter.

"*A*. So *BA*."

Esther signed again. Mary grinned. "Another *B*? *BAB*?"

By now, everyone in the family was watching the exchange. Esther signed the next letter.

"I'm not sure about that one. Let me look it up." Mary thumbed through the book Esther had given her to study.

"*Y*," she announced. "*B.A.B.Y.* Your announcement is—baby?"

Esther nodded and blushed a pretty shade of pink.

"You're having a baby? That's *wunderbar*! I'm so happy for you." Mary jumped out of her chair to hug the mother-to-be.

Talitha put her knitting aside with a beaming smile. "Is this true? When? A grandbaby! My prayers have been answered."

Gabe slipped his arm around Esther's shoulders. "Early November we think."

Pamela rushed to her sister, and the two women embraced. Mary stepped back. Seth came over to pump Gabe's hand. "Congratulations. This is wonderful news, but you stole my thunder."

Gabe looked puzzled. Then he grinned. "You, too?"

Pamela slid her arm around Seth's waist. "October with our Lord's blessing. Esther and I agreed that she and Gabe should announce it first because he is the eldest."

"We'll need to start building you your own homes now," Zeke said with a wide grin. "I'm going to a *grossdaadi*. Daadi. I like the sound of that."

"I'm going to be an *onkel*." Moses grinned from ear to ear. "Women love men who like babies. I'll babysit whenever you need me."

"Great," Gabe said. "Mamm can teach you how to change dirty diapers. There'll be a lot of them with two infants in the house."

Moses's grin faded. "I might watch them when they're older."

Seth and Gabe burst out laughing. Ash smiled, but he couldn't help a twinge of envy. His brothers were moving into new territory. He would be excluded more than ever. They would be fathers. They would have their own homes.

The idea that having a wife might somehow keep him close to his brothers seemed ridiculous now. It couldn't be one for all and all for one with the three of them anymore. They were meant to grow apart. It was only natural that they lead different lives. Even if Mary agreed to marry him, it wouldn't change that.

He watched her smiling and congratulating his family. He didn't want what his brothers had now. He wanted Mary to be part of his life because he was falling in love with her. Not with some vague, inaccurate idea of her, but with the flesh-and-blood woman he saw before him. He wanted to walk his own path, the one the Lord had chosen for him, with her at his side.

Gabe walked over and stood in front of Ash. "Did we leave you speechless?"

"You did." Ash smiled, got to his feet, drew

his brother into a bear hug and pounded his back. Seth came over. Ash wrapped one arm around him. "You two as fathers. It boggles the mind. Your poor *kinder*. Thank the Lord you both have responsible, bright wives to correct all the mistakes you'll make."

"So true," Pamela said, signing for Esther who laughed.

After congratulations went all around, Ash noticed Mary slip out into the garden. He followed her. She crossed to the rose arbor and took a seat on the bench. She seemed lost in thought. He walked over. "May I join you?"

She looked up with a soft smile. "Please do."

He sat and clasped his hands tightly together because he wanted to put his arm around her. "Happy news."

"Your *mamm* looked overjoyed. Your *daed* looked a bit stunned."

"I'm not sure he's ready to be a *grossdaadi*."

"How are you feeling?"

He looked down and chuckled. "I believe that's usually a question I ask you."

"Turnabout is fair play."

"I'm happy for them and grateful to *Gott* for this gift to our family. And you? You were looking pretty serious when I came out here."

"I was battling envy. It seems my husband and I weren't blessed with children. It must have pained us both. I would have loved to be a mother."

"It's not out of the question. You're young."

She cocked her head to the side. "How old did you say I am? Isn't it sad that I need to ask you instead of just knowing? When is my birthday? Did I have one and missed it?"

"You're twenty-nine. I have no idea when your birthday is."

"So I could be thirty even if I told you the truth."

"Of course you told me the truth."

"Not all of it. Maybe I fudged my age to sound more eligible."

"You don't look thirty. Except when you're looking haggard and worn. Then you look thirty-five, six, seven."

She fell against him laughing. "Ash, you are the best friend I've ever had. I'm sure of that even if I can't recall any other. You're the only person who can make me laugh by being rude."

A blush rose to her cheeks. She moved away and looked down.

"You should try insulting me in return. It's kind of fun," he suggested, hoping she would smile again. He loved her smile and her lilting laugh.

Keeping her eyes lowered, she shook her head.

"I could never insult you. You've done too much for me. I'm so very grateful."

He didn't want her gratitude. He wanted her to like him for himself. "Forget about anything you think I've done."

Her gaze flew to his. "I pray to *Gott* I never forget a single thing about you."

Ash raised his face to the heavens. "That was a poor choice of words on my part." He glanced at her. "I'm sorry."

A smile crept across her lips. "Haggard and worn? I don't think saying *forget* is the poor choice you have to apologize for."

"Okay, I'm sorry for saying you look thirty-seven."

"Have you always been impossible?"

He got to his feet and held out his hand. "You'll have to ask my mother. Come back in. I think I saw Esther sign that she and Pamela made cake."

Mary grasped his hand and stood. "Cake sounds lovely."

Warmth spread from his hand holding hers until it filled his heart. He gazed in amazement at how beautiful she looked in the evening light. Her pupils darkened as her eyes widened. What was she thinking? Did she feel it too, this current that swirled, surrounded them like electricity?

What would she say if he asked to kiss her? Would she shyly agree or be horrified?

She lowered her eyes, breaking the connection between them. In that moment, he knew. He wanted her in his arms. Longed to kiss her sweet lips, to tell her she was beautiful in every way and that he thanked God for bringing them together.

She slowly slipped her fingers from his and the moment passed. She stepped away and went into the house. Missing her touch with a physical ache, he lingered for a moment to gather his composure. He never imagined it would be this difficult to remain her friend.

He fixed a smile on his face and went to join the celebration with his family.

Mary accepted a plate of cake from Talitha and moved to sit in the chair at the desk in the corner. Ash took his plate and stood across the room. Mary glanced his way once and then concentrated on her food. Something had passed between them in the garden. It changed her, made her deeply aware of him in a way she didn't know was possible.

She looked up and found him watching her. It wasn't friendship she read in his dark eyes. A deeper emotion pulled her toward him. It was frightening and exciting at the same time.

She looked away. Nothing could come of it. She couldn't allow it.

The front door opened, and Bishop Schultz came in. He greeted everyone, but his face was grim.

"Welcome, Bishop," Zeke said. "Come in and have some cake."

"I can't stay, *danki*. I've had word from Mary's bishop. I thought she would want to know. May I speak to her?"

Mary stood up. "Of course."

The bishop glanced around the room. "Should we talk in private?"

She couldn't look at Ash. "The Fisher family deserves to know what you have learned."

"As you wish." He pulled a letter from his pocket. "You were placed under the Bann for lack of humility, dishonesty in a financial matter, for defying your bishop and your failure to repent these sins."

"I don't see how that's possible," Talitha said. "Mary isn't like that. What are the details of her supposed dishonesty? He must have written more than that?"

The bishop waved the paper in his hand. "I'm afraid this is all he said. Mary, do you repent these sins?"

Even now, she had no real idea what she had done or why. Bowing her head, she nodded. "I do."

"Then my judgement has not changed. You are welcome here."

"I appreciate you coming by Bishop Schultz." She held her head up as she walked out of the living room.

Ash followed and caught her by the arm. "Mary, wait."

She couldn't bear to look into his eyes and see his disappointment. She fled up the stairs. Leaning against the door of her bedroom, she let her tears run down her face. Now Ash and everyone knew what kind of person she was.

The following day, overcast gray skies gave way to heavy rain. Mary stared out her bedroom window at the puddles growing in the gravel yard between the house and barn. The horses in the corral stood with their heads down and their tails toward the north wind, but they didn't seem to mind it enough to go into their dry stalls.

The entire family had gone to share their good news with close friends. Would they be sharing her story, too? No, she didn't believe that. They were too kind for that sort of gossip.

She should go stand in the rain. It couldn't be more miserable than doing nothing but thinking and wondering. Dishonesty, lack of humility, defying the bishop. As hard as she tried to remember the things she had done, all she accomplished was making her headache worse.

She had wanted to avoid the sorrow-filled faces of the Fisher family. Having endured enough of that at breakfast, she had pleaded a headache afterward and returned to her room, so she didn't have to go with them. They'd been trying their best to make her feel welcome and forgiven, but she just felt more like a fraud. She was a dishonest, prideful woman who had schemed to marry Ash.

Dearest Ash. Maybe it hadn't been a complete lie. Perhaps she had developed feelings for him from the letters he wrote. She could imagine them. He would've written about the farm, the family business and his brothers. It was possible she liked what she read and thought they would make a good match. It was less painful to believe that than thinking she had deliberately deceived him. Had she turned to him because she had no one else?

Ever since she woke up in the hospital, she had sensed something special between them. Something more than friendship. Ash had been there when she needed comfort the most. It was possible she had read more into his friendliness because she wanted to.

Those feelings had to stay buried. She wasn't right for him. He deserved so much better.

The patter of the raindrops on the window drew her attention again. What she needed was a walk in the rain. It always helped.

Mary inhaled sharply. *The rain. She used to walk in the rain.*

Racing downstairs, she flew out the door into the farmyard. Cold rain soaked her head and dress in a matter of moments as she turned in a circle, then strolled toward the barn. The smell of the rain and wet earth brought unexpected comfort in spite of the cold. She lifted her face to the sky and let the water cascade over her face.

"I hate getting wet, Daed. Please hurry."

"Nonsense." His laughter boomed as he held his arms wide. *"We can't get any wetter than we already are. Lift your face to* Gott's *blessing and let it renew your soul the way it renews the earth."*

"Mary, what are you doing?" Ash was covering her with a blanket that smelled like a horse.

She grinned. "I'm listening to my *daed*. I hear his voice."

Ash bundled her toward the barn. "You're freezing. Let's get you out of the rain. You shouldn't get that cast wet."

She looked at her arm. "I forgot about my cast. I like walking in the rain. He liked being in the rain."

"I don't." He pulled her into the workshop

and led her to the glowing forge. He pumped the bellows, and the coals grew bright red. He pulled a bench over. "Sit here. This will get you warmed up."

Now that she was out of the rain she started to shiver. "I heard my father's voice, Ash. I remember a day with him." She could barely get the words out between her chattering teeth.

"We were riding home on the wagon. We got caught in a shower. I was miserable and told him to hurry. He laughed. Sa-said we couldn't get any wetter than we already were. He had a wonderful booming bi-big laugh, but I can't see his face."

She looked at Ash. "I want to see him again, but you said he died. I want to remember more things about him, but I can't. There's nothing else." She dropped to her knees and began sobbing. "I hate this. I hate it."

"It'll be okay. Hush now." Ash's gentle words pierced her sorrow. He wrapped the blanket firmly around her, lifted her from the floor and cradled her beside the warm forge.

Resting against his shoulder was wonderfully comforting. Her sobs died away into occasional hiccups. He didn't say anything more. He just held her. She never wanted to move.

Sandwiched between his warmth and the heat of the fire, her shivers lessened until they stopped altogether. There was only the sound of the rain on the roof, the smell of smoke and the strength of his arms around her.

"How come you aren't with your family?"

"I didn't want you to be here alone."

She loved his compassion. "Why is this happening to me, Ash?"

"I don't know. It must be part of a greater plan because *Gott* allows it." There was so much sympathy in his soft words. It brought more tears to her eyes.

"He shouldn't," she mumbled.

"His reasons are beyond our understanding."

She sniffled. "I'm angry with Him for doing this to me."

Ash stroked her hair. "So am I, darling."

That drove a spike into her heart. "How can you call me that after what you know about me?"

"Oh, Mary, I can't change how I feel."

"You should. It's the only reasonable thing to do."

"That's not going to happen. I like you very much."

"No, you don't. You feel sorry for me." She scrambled away and ran to the house. In the safety of her room, she sat down on the bed and stared at the floor. Despite everything he knew, Ash still liked her. He had called her darling. Because he felt sorry for her or because he meant it?

She pulled the curtain aside and looked out her window. He was standing in the rain staring up at her.

What if he really meant it?

Chapter Ten

Mary remained in her room for the rest of the day with her hair down so it would dry. Brushing it soothed her. She wasn't hiding, but she wasn't ready to face Ash, either. Pamela brought a tray of food at suppertime. After that, no one pressed her to come out.

That night she dreamed she was again standing in the rain, only the water was rising quickly around her. The rain came in torrents. She had nowhere to go. She saw Ash trying to wade toward her. The current kept pushing him away. Crying out she reached for him, but the water closed over him, and he vanished. She woke sobbing and shivering. Huddled beneath the quilt, Mary knew it hadn't simply been a dream. Some part of it was true.

Early the next morning, there was a knock on her door. Talitha looked in. "Today is the school frolic, Mary. They're expecting your help." She shut the door without waiting for Mary's reply.

Was she ready to face the family and community? Mary pulled the quilt over her head. Silly question. Ash was the one she was afraid to confront. What if he'd realized he'd made a mistake yesterday?

What if he *meant* his words? What if he did care for her?

Knowing she wouldn't learn the truth in her room, she threw back the covers, dressed, pinned her *kapp* on straight and went down to face him. The men, except for Zeke, were already gone. It was a welcome reprieve.

An hour later, Zeke Fisher turned the family's buggy into the schoolyard and stopped the team beside the hitching rail out front. A half-dozen others were already lined up there. Ash and his brothers had arrived earlier and were beside a small barn unloading lumber from their wagon. It would be used to build additional playground equipment and benches for the ball diamond.

Mary watched them for a few minutes. It amazed her how handsome Ash looked in the early morning light. Dressed as the other men were in dark pants with suspenders, blue long-sleeved shirts and straw hats, there was nothing to make him stand out, and yet he did. She could pick him out of a hundred men or more.

He caught sight of her and smiled. She waved and felt the heat rush to her cheeks. Then she chided herself for acting like a smitten schoolgirl and quickly looked away, only to catch Pamela and Esther watching her with knowing smiles. Had Ash told them about his feelings for her? The sisters quickly sobered and continued unpacking the buggy.

Mary turned her attention to the school. The white one-story building with a steep roof had large windows across both sides of the building and a bell tower at the front. It sat back a dozen yards from the road. The playground consisted of a large patch of close-cut grass, A-frame swing set with four swings, a teeter-totter and a softball field with a chain-link backstop. Four young boys were throwing a ball around the bases.

Zeke went to confer with Bishop Schultz on what needed to be done. Talitha handed her basket to a young man who bore a striking resemblance to Eva Gingrich. "Welcome. We're glad you could make it. The women are gathered inside."

He helped Talitha and then Mary down. "I'm Danny Coblentz, the teacher. You must be Mary. I hope you're enjoying your stay with the Fishers. New Covenant has a lot to offer Amish folks interested in moving here."

"It certainly is beautiful." The school grounds backed up to the dense woods. A light breeze brought a piney scent that was mixed with another fragrance she couldn't identify. "What is that smell?"

He frowned for a second and then laughed. "Potato blossoms. The whole valley is covered with them this time of year. It's the main crop in our county."

One of the boys on the field yelled his name. Danny excused himself and jogged away to see what his student wanted.

Talitha leaned close to Mary. "He's a single fellow. He earns a nice living from the school board. The position comes with that sweet little house." She nodded to the home next door.

Mary rolled her eyes. "Am I going to be introduced to every unattached fellow in the community today?"

Talitha looked horrified. "Of course not. Several of them have jobs elsewhere and can't be here today. Danny is a good catch though. My cousin Waneta had high hopes for him and her daughter Julia, but sadly they fell out. Oh, there's Dinah. I must speak to her."

"Talitha?"

She looked back. "Yes?"

"Did Ash say anything about me yesterday?"

"He said you got caught out in the rain. Was there something else?"

"*Nee*, never mind."

"All right. I'll be in soon." She went to join her friend.

Mary picked up the last basket and carried it into the building. The school itself was a single room with wide, scuffed plank floors. Dust motes drifted in the beams of sunlight shining through the south-facing windows. At the front of the room was a raised platform with the teacher's desk. A dusty blackboard covered the wall behind it. Off to the side was a large bookcase completely crammed full of books. The student desks had been pushed against the walls. They would be taken outside to be cleaned while the ceiling, floor and walls were scrubbed.

The women of the community were gathered at the front. Eva Gingrich seemed to be in charge, dividing up the tasks and handing out supplies.

Mary walked up to the group. "What would you like me to do?"

Eva smiled at her. "I'm glad you could make it. Why don't you help Dinah and Gemma get the food ready and put out when it's time to eat? We have tables set up on the north side of the building. We'll clean the school this morning and then work in the house this afternoon. Please don't feel you have to stay and help the entire day. The house is open. Gemma is there making coffee. You might see if she needs help right now."

On her way out, Mary almost ran into a man carrying in a large box. She held the door open for him. He was tall and thin with a narrow face, close-set dark eyes and a hawk nose. He stopped to scowl at her. "You're new here."

She smiled. "I am. I'm visiting the Fisher family."

His expression brightened. "You're the one with amnesia. I was sorry to hear about your accident. The *Englisch* drive much too fast and have little regard for our people and especially our horses and buggies. Are you thinking of staying in New Covenant?"

"I'm afraid it's too soon for me to say that with any certainty."

He grinned and leaned toward her. "I'm Jedidiah Zook, by the way. Look forward to seeing you again. I plan to stop in and visit the Fishers real soon."

"I'm sure they are always happy to welcome a friend of the family." She slipped out the door and headed to the adjacent house.

Gemma was waiting for her on the porch. "I see you met Jedidiah. Did he say he'd drop by the Fishers' for a visit?"

Mary cocked her head. "As a matter of fact he did."

"You have sparked his interest."

Mary frowned over her shoulder. "Is he one of the fellows Talitha has lined up?"

Gemma contemplated the idea. "He might be. His brother- and sister-in-law in Pennsylvania recently died in a buggy accident and their two daughters have come to live with him. I pity them."

Intrigued, Mary eyed Gemma. "Why is that?"

"Oh, there's nothing wrong with the man. He's a successful farmer, but he doesn't have much personality. If you're looking for a no-nonsense, boring fellow with a big farm, he's your man."

"A big farm?" Mary giggled. "Then he definitely goes to the top. Oh, I shouldn't say that even in jest." Ash was the only man she wanted on Talitha's list.

Gemma took Mary's arm. "I can't see you settling for boring. The coffee is almost done. Would you mind taking some around to the men putting in the new playground equipment?"

Mary knew that was where Ash was working. She couldn't think of a reason to refuse. The truth was, she was eager to see him. She needed to know if his feelings had changed.

With a carafe of hot coffee in hand, she found a card table set up beside the barn. Someone had laid out foam cups, plastic spoons, sugar and a small pitcher of cream. Gemma followed her with a platter of baked goods. The men came up one at a time to get their coffee and rolls. Ash was among the last to make his way over.

She handed him a cup and his fingers closed around hers sending her pulse racing. This rush of emotion was not her imagination. They stared at each other until Gabe cleared his throat behind Ash.

Giving herself a quick mental shake, Mary stepped to the side. "Coffee, Gabe?"

"Danki." He took a cup and walked away after nudging Ash with his elbow.

Ash ignored his brother and stood sipping his drink by the table. She struggled to find something to say. Finally, she looked at the wooden climbing area they were building. "How is it going?"

"You should know I don't feel sorry for anyone. I only hope things can progress from here. What about you?"

His eyes were filled with a soft expression that warmed her to her toes. Smiling, she looked down. "I think that could happen."

"Seriously? I'm mighty glad to hear you say that."

Gemma giggled and held out her platter. "Would you like a sticky bun, or is Mary the only sweet you're after?"

Ash blushed a deep red. "Thanks for the coffee." He hurried back to where his brothers were working.

Gemma gathered up the empty cups. "The two of you weren't talking about building the playground equipment."

Mary tried to bluff. "Of course we were."

"Nope. That man was looking at you the way Jesse still looks at me, and you were looking back."

Mary sighed. "I was, wasn't I?"

She had fought it long enough. She was falling in love with Asher Ethan Fisher. Admitting it to herself was freeing.

The rest of the day she enjoyed visiting with the women, helping keep track of the small children and watching Ash.

Bishop Schultz put him in charge of painting the small barn and corral fences. His crew of helpers were five boys ranging in age from six to ten. Ash patiently showed the youngers what needed to be done, helping the smallest one to hold his brush correctly and even lifting one child so he could paint the underside of the eves. Despite the amount of paint that landed on his clothes, he continually encouraged and praised the boy's work.

When the picnic-style lunch was served, he brought his plate over to where Mary sat in the shade with two infants. One on her lap and one on the quilt. He sank onto the ground next to her. "Who do you have there?"

"Charity and Jacob Weaver."

"Ah, the lumberjack's twins."

"Maisie asked me to watch them while she gets some food. Aren't they adorable? I love their red hair."

"Have you eaten?"

"I'll get something in a bit. I'm rather occupied at the moment." Jacob was up on his knees, crawling toward the edge of the quilt. Mary was trying to wrest a bug out of Charity's hand before she got it into her mouth.

Ash rescued Jacob and deposited him in the center of the quilt. The baby immediately headed in the other direction. Ash snatched him up again and settled the child on his lap. Unwilling to sit still, Jacob tried to climb up Ash's chest using his suspender. "Where is Moses when you need a babysitter?"

He looked completely at ease with a baby in his arms. "You must like children." Mary tossed the liberated bug away. "I saw you overseeing the paint crew."

"I do like kids. I look forward to being an *onkel*."

"And a father?"

He smiled at her. "Someday if all goes well."

* * *

Mary decided she and Ash were like two children sharing a special secret at breakfast the next morning. Every time she looked at him, he was smiling at her. She grinned at him, too, but quickly lowered her eyes hoping no one else noticed. It was a forlorn hope. Esther and Pamela exchanged little comments in sign and giggled.

Gabe winked at her. "Beautiful morning, isn't it, Ash?"

"*Ja*, beautiful." His comment was followed by the rumble of thunder. Seth choked on a sip of coffee. Gabe pounded his back.

Ash scowled at his brothers. "What? We could use more rain."

"We will take what *Gott* sends," Zeke declared. "We've plenty of work to keep us busy inside the shop. We should get started. *Goot* meal, Mudder." He rose to his feet. Seth and Gabe did as well. Moses stuffed one more biscuit in his mouth and went out with them.

Ash rose. "I'll be in the shop when you're ready to go to Naomi's. I'll hitch up the buggy first thing."

They would be alone together on the ride to the sanctuary. Mary clenched her fingers together to still her jitters. "I'll be out when our morning chores are done."

After he left, Mary began humming as she

helped gather up the dishes. She stopped when she discovered Talitha gazing at her with a self-satisfied smile. "What?"

Talitha raised both hands in the air. "I'm not saying anything. Except, sometimes I'm right even when other people refuse to see that."

Mary didn't reply. She hurried through her share of the housework and then gathered a few supplies to take along to Naomi's house.

When she stepped out the door, she saw Ash was already waiting by the buggy. "I thought you were working in the shop?"

"Daed said I wasn't much use this morning. There was too much joking going on." He looked over his shoulder. Mary noticed all three of his brothers gathered in the doorway waving to them.

"Shall we go?" She hurried into the buggy. Her face had to be beet red.

Once they were out on the highway, she relaxed. The clip-clop of the horse's feet on the roadway and the jingle of the harness filled the quiet morning as they drove along. The storm clouds moved off. The sun came out making the raindrops on everything sparkle.

Ash cleared his throat. "I think we should talk about this."

"This what?" She waited to exhale.

He glanced at her. "Us."

She let out the breath she'd been holding. Why was she so nervous? "You mean our friendship?"

"Mary, I think we both know this has moved past friendship."

"What if it has? Nothing has changed except I know more about why I was shunned." Was she foolish to believe he could overlook that?

"I know those things trouble you. But none of that matters to me."

What wonderful words. Her heart filled with joy. She had to trust that God brought Ash into her life for a reason if she was going to take a chance on happiness. "I reckon if you can forgive my poor behavior, maybe I can look to the future instead of trying to see into the past."

He reached over and grasped her hand. "Does this mean you'll walk out with me?"

She nodded. "I believe it does."

His bright smile warmed her heart. "You won't be sorry, Mary."

Sitting up straighter, she looked ahead. "I have one condition."

He pulled his hand away. "Okay."

"You'll have to stop being rude to me."

"What do you mean? Oh, so I can't say you look haggard and worn-out anymore?" He jiggled the driving lines to speed up the horse.

"That's right."

He chuckled. "I can't tell folks your age might be thirty-eight or thirty-nine?"

Outraged, she stared at him with her mouth open. "Absolutely not."

"And no jokes about forgetting the color of the sky or how to count to ten?"

"Are you done?" She tried to sound miffed but couldn't.

"Sure. I won't use any of those innocent comments that you consider rude."

She turned her face away. "I believe I just forgot I was going to walk out with you."

He nudged her with his shoulder. "*Nee*, you didn't."

Casting him a sidelong glance, she knew she hadn't fooled him. "What makes you so sure?"

"Because of the way your eyes sparkle when you look at me."

She grew serious. "I pray my past never hurts you, Ash."

He covered her hand with his own and gave a gentle squeeze. "It won't."

"Then there is one more thing you need to know right now."

"It won't make a difference in how I feel." His earnest expression warmed her heart.

"I'm glad, but you just missed the turn to Naomi's place."

Chuckling, he slowed Dottie and brought her around. "I was wrong. Now I feel foolish."

Remarkable happiness churned in Mary. How was it possible to feel so blessed only two days after her darkest hour?

Ash had no intention of dropping Mary off at Naomi's and returning home. He hadn't needed to confide in his brothers. Apparently, his feelings were plainly written on his face. At their urging and with his father's consent, he had the rest of the day off to woo Mary. He wasn't going to waste it.

Naomi was in her front yard with her dog and eight ducks. Mary got out of the buggy and turned to him. "I wish you didn't have to leave."

"I don't. I am at Naomi's disposal for the day."

Naomi was trying to encourage her ducks into a pen. The ducks had other ideas. "That's a welcome surprise. I could use a hand right now."

It took the three of them twenty minutes and numerous attempts, several foiled by the dog's unwelcome assistance, to finally secure all eight ducks in their enclosure. Ash bent over with his hands braced on his knees and tried to catch his breath.

Naomi was panting as hard as the dog. "Mama Fox got one of them last night. After this, I just might leave the gate open tonight."

"You don't mean that." Mary crouched beside the wire fence and let one duck nibble at her fingers through the wire.

"Let's just say I'm tempted."

Mary looked up at her. "Does that mean Trouble's mother is still coming around?"

"I can't be sure it was her last night, but I think so. I wish I knew where her den is. I would like to release Trouble near there when he's well enough."

"Mary and I can do some scouting later. We've seen her twice near our farm. I have a general idea."

Planting her hands on her hips, Naomi leaned back and stretched. "I'm too old for this."

Laughing, Mary stood up. "That's why you hired me."

"And why I'm here for free," Ash said.

Naomi arched one eyebrow. "I don't think you're here just to help an old lady, Ash, but I'll take what I can get."

Ash figured he was blushing, but he didn't care if Naomi knew how much he liked Mary. He wanted everyone to know. "Where should I start?"

She held up her arms and turned around. "Take your pick. The fence needs fixing and painting. A hinge came loose on the barn door. The weeds are getting taller than the dog. Have at it."

"And me?" Mary asked.

"Clean the cages in the barn. Don't let any of the animals out while you're doing it. I'm not going to run after another creature this morning." She headed into the house.

Ash folded his arms over his chest. "Are you sure you want to work for her?"

"Absolutely. I even brought rubber gloves and overshoes."

"Then the sooner we get started the sooner we'll be done, and we can go looking for Trouble's home. I wonder if Naomi has any paint for her picket fence?"

Mary had some trouble managing the cage cleaning with only one good arm. Twice she had to get Ash to help her. He willingly dropped whatever he was doing and came to her aid.

She had been afraid that agreeing to date would impact their friendship, but she didn't see any trace of that. They were even better friends now that she didn't have to hide how she felt.

Naomi fixed them a lunch of wild rice with fresh mushrooms, a green salad from her garden and mixed-berry tarts for dessert. Then she brought out three paintbrushes, two oversized shirts to cover their clothes and a can of paint. Mary had to wonder if she had ever enjoyed an afternoon so much.

When the fence was done and left to dry, Ash

took a walk around Naomi's duck pen and went a little way into the woods.

"I've found her trail," he said when he came back. "Are you too tired for a hike, Mary?"

Too exhausted to take a walk alone in the woods with Ash? She shook her head. "I'm not the least bit tired."

Naomi chuckled. "If you aren't back in an hour, I'll send a search party."

"We'll be back," Ash assured her without taking his eyes off Mary.

"Do look for the vixen's den while you're out there." She gave him a hard stare.

Ash stood up straight. "Yes, ma'am. We'll be back in an hour with a location where we can release Trouble."

He walked away from the sharp eyes of Naomi with Mary at his side.

It was cool in the woods. The ground was damp after the recent rains and held the footprints of numerous forest creatures. Backtracking the fox wasn't difficult. Occasional white duck feathers proved they were going in the right direction. The trees opened out into a small clearing with a pond in the center. Just at the edge of the forest stood a jumble of granite boulders. A few more duck feathers in front of a group of low shrubs told him the den had to be behind them.

"Let's wait and see if anyone is about," he whispered.

Mary looked around with wide eyes. "What a perfect place for a home. The reflection of the trees and sky in the pond is like a mirror. I can't imagine anything prettier."

Ash turned her face toward him with a finger under her chin. "I don't have to imagine. I'm looking at something much prettier."

Her eyes darkened. "I think you should kiss me now."

"My thoughts exactly." He leaned forward and covered her lips with his own. He meant it to be a brief, chaste kiss, but the moment he tasted the sweetness of her, that plan went out of his head.

Chapter Eleven

Mary knew his kiss would be wonderful. The touch of his warm mouth against hers sent her mind reeling. The sounds of the woods faded away. There was nothing but the need to be in his arms. His firm lips pressed against hers, tenderly at first, but growing more insistent as his arms encircled her to pull her close. She cupped his face with her hand and ran her fingers up into his hair, adoring the silky softness of it. His hat fell off and landed in the grass. She didn't care. She just wanted to hold him, be held by him and float together on the wonderous sensation of joy.

When he pulled away, she came drifting back to earth.

He tucked her head under his chin. His breathing was as unsteady as hers. "I think we should head back."

"Why?" She didn't want the moment to end. Had she ever felt this way before?

"Our hour will be up soon. I firmly believe Naomi will send out a search party."

A soft sigh escaped her tingling lips. "You're right. I don't think she makes idle threats. I'm sorry we didn't see the foxes."

"I have a feeling they saw us first. It's hard to sneak up on a fox. They have big ears."

"And sharp eyes."

"And excellent noses. They will know we've been here if they didn't see us. Are you ready to go back?"

"Nee."

He cocked his head to the side with a smug grin on his face. "Did you forget the way?"

She jerked away from him. "You promised you wouldn't be rude to me anymore."

"Did I promise that?"

"You did." Frowning, she took a step away.

He caught her hand and pulled her back into his embrace. "Then I'm sorry. My mind is a muddle when I'm near you. Do you forgive me?"

How could she not? "I guess. On one condition."

"Another condition?"

She felt the rumble of his laugh deep in his chest. A sly grin curved her lips. "You'll like this one."

"Okay, what is it?"

"One more kiss."

"Don't the *Englisch* call that blackmail? But you're right. I do like your condition." He leaned toward her. Closing her eyes she raised her face. He planted a kiss on her forehead.

She pursed her lips in a pout. "That was not what I had in mind."

"But it's all you get." He took her hand. "Come on. Naomi is waiting for us."

With her hand in his, Mary walked along the trail, cocooned in contentment, surrounded by the earthy fragrance of the mossy woods she loved. She gazed up at the man beside her and wondered where this relationship was heading. How could she let it go further without repairing the damage she had done to her family and community back home?

He squeezed her hand. "What has you so deep in thought, Mary?"

"The past."

"I expected that."

"My shunning will always be a blight on my reputation, even if I'm accepted into the New Covenant church. We both know it won't remain a secret, and it shouldn't."

"What can you do?"

"I'm going to write to my in-laws. Tell them I'm sorry, that I repent and ask forgiveness. I'll ask to speak with them on the phone and hope they agree. Maybe hearing their voices will trigger some kind of recognition."

Ash squeezed her hand. "I think that's a fine idea. You can dictate it to me. I'll write it for you if that's acceptable."

She smiled at him. "*Danki*, that would be a great help. I might be able to scratch a note with my left hand, but I doubt anyone could read it."

It felt good to have a plan and to share it with Ash.

When they came out of the woods, they saw Naomi was indeed waiting on them. Seated in a rocker on her porch, she gave the impression of a ruffled mother hen. "About time. I have Search and Rescue on speed dial, you know."

"We're back safe and sound," Ash said. "We followed the trail of your visitor last night to a pond about a mile into the woods."

"I know the place. Be here tomorrow at noon, Mary." She rose from her chair to go in the house but stopped in the doorway and looked back. "You both did a fine job today. I appreciate it. Thanks." She went inside. The dog followed her.

Ash raised both his eyebrows. "A compliment from Naomi Walker. Those don't get handed out every day."

"You're too hard on her, Ash. She's a sweet lady. I wish I knew why she seems familiar."

"No more visions or flashes of memories?"

"None."

He folded his arms across his chest and stared at his feet. "I thought maybe when we kissed that you might remember kissing your husband."

She laid her hand on his arm. "*Nee*, I only thought how wonderful it was to kiss you."

Looking relieved, he grinned. "Then maybe we should try it again."

"First you'll take me home and help me write my letter. Ash, I need to reconcile with my church, my husband's family, my friends. You understand, don't you?"

"I'm not making any demands on you. Where we go from here is completely dependent on what you're comfortable with."

"You're a marvelous friend."

"Could you put *boy* in front of that?"

"You're a marvelous boyfriend."

He grinned. "I try. Let's go home and write your letter."

Mary pushed aside the sudden fear that gripped her. It was the right thing to do. She couldn't move forward until she had repaired what she could of her past, so why was she afraid?

Ash helped Mary craft a brief but sincere apology to her in-laws, asking them to set a time when they could speak on the phone. After putting the letter in the mailbox, she turned to him with a broad smile. "I feel like I'm finally taking control of my life. Now we just wait."

"I admire your determination to reconcile with them." Ash didn't care if they accepted Mary's peace offering or not. But it was important to her. He was prepared to wait until she was ready to take the next step in their relationship, but the memory of the kiss they shared kept him awake at night.

What didn't make him happy was to see Jedidiah Zook show up on Sunday for a visit. He claimed he was taking his two nieces around to meet the other families in the district, but Ash saw Jed had his eyes on Mary.

The nieces were ten and eleven, somber, subdued children who seemed lost. Perhaps that was to be expected after losing both parents. Mary spent much of Jedidiah's visit talking to them and getting them to open up. Ash was amazed at her compassion and persistence. It was her story about the fox that caught their interest.

"She keeps a fox in her barn?" Lydia was the older of the two.

"It's the truth. A baby fox with an injured leg. His name is Trouble."

The younger girl, Polly, smiled sadly. "That was our *daed's* nickname for me."

Mary laid a hand on the child's head. "Then

you must come and meet Trouble. You are twins. He had red hair and so do you."

Polly turned to Jedidiah. "May we go see the fox, Onkel Jed?"

"If Mary has time one of these days. I'm sure we'd all enjoy spending more time with her."

Mary's smile slipped a little. "I'll have to check with Naomi."

When the visit was finally over, Ash accompanied Jed out to his buggy. The girls were saying goodbye to his family. He drew himself up to his full height, a good four inches taller than Jed. "I think you should know Mary is walking out with me."

Jed frowned. "I see. She seems like a nice woman. It's just that my nieces are going to need a mother. I don't know anything about raising girls. I can't teach them the things they need to know. If it doesn't work between the two of you, will you let me know?"

Ash learned he could experience jealousy and compassion in the same moment. He managed a smile. "Don't hold your breath, Jed. It'll work out for us. I'm sure of it."

Mary rode beside Ash on the seat of the family's wagon the next afternoon. He had several rolls of chicken wire, garden fencing and eight posts to build additional pens beside the barn so that some of the animals could enjoy the fresh air and sunshine.

When they reached the turnoff to Naomi's lane, Mary tapped his arm. "Stop a minute, please."

He did. She got down to examine the donation box. "We definitely need a larger sign here."

"I think I can find some scrap boards that will work. In fact, I think I saw several behind Naomi's barn if she'll let us use them. A bigger sign might bring more animals as well as more donations. We should make sure she wants that."

"You're right." Mary tried to climb back up, but found she needed both arms.

"Step back," Ash said and jumped down when she was out of the way. "Come here." He motioned her closer.

Stepping behind her, he grasped her waist and lifted her up to the wagon seat. She gritted her teeth at the pain in her rib but kept a smile on her face. Her heart took a minute to settle down. He was so strong and gentle. She struggled to cover the effect he had on her. "I will be glad to get this cast off."

"How much longer?" He came around the wagon and got in on his side.

"The doctor said x-ray in four more weeks. Then I will know if it's healing right."

He drove up to the house and stopped the wagon beside the barn. It took him only a few minutes to unload, then he went to explore some of Naomi's scattered outbuildings.

Naomi opened the barn door. "I thought I heard someone out here. What's all this?"

"Ash is going to build some new pens for you. We thought you could use a bigger sign at the donation box, too, but wanted to check with you first."

"If he wants to do that, I guess that's okay."

"What name do you want on the sign?" Mary asked.

Naomi shrugged. "You think of something. Come with me."

Mary followed Naomi inside the barn. The little fox was pacing in a smaller cage.

"Why is he back in here?" Mary asked.

"I'm going to remove his cast and replace it with a splint. He'll have to be tranquilized. I don't want him struggling."

"Can I help?"

"You can. I'm not going to put him under deeply, but I will need you to watch and make sure he's still breathing or that he isn't waking up."

Naomi administered the drug with a small dart gun and waited until the kit leaned against the side of the crate and then slumped to the floor. The outside door opened. Ash came in.

"What are we doing?"

"Removing his cast," Mary told him.

"Ash, bring him over here," Naomi said. She stood beside a white folding table. Mary helped Ash slide the baby out of the kennel without hurting his leg and brought him to Naomi's workstation.

She handed her stethoscope to Mary. "Listen and tap out what you're hearing with your finger. That way I can see what his heart rate is. Ash, bring that little cutting wheel over here. Now hold his leg out straight for me."

Ash did as he was instructed while Mary tapped out to the baby's heart rate. It remained steady and strong until Naomi finished her work. She picked up her tools. "Go ahead and put him back, Ash. I need someone to sit with him until he comes around."

"I'll do it." Mary stroked the kit's thick, soft pelt.

"I'll stay with you," Ash said.

Mary smiled at him. "Don't you have a pen to build?"

"I'll get to it." He pulled up a folding chair that Naomi had leaning against the wall and brought over a three-legged stool for himself.

They sat beside each other in the quiet barn without speaking. The smell of animals, hay and old barn wood scented the air. Dust moats danced in the light shafts that came in through the gaps in the siding and the small windows. It was wonderfully peaceful and cozy. Mary was sorry when the little fox began to stir and sat up.

She stretched. "Did you find some wood for a sign?"

"Wood and blue paint, if that works."

"Sounds perfect. Let's go."

She felt like skipping as they walked along the lane. It was a carefree kind of day. She realized she hadn't struggled to recall a memory even once. She was coming to grips with the fact that her memory might not return ever. She glanced at Ash. She was making new memories just as he said she would.

They sketched out the sign in the dirt, deciding the lettering in size. They settled on Walker Animal Sanctuary. Ash nailed up the board while Mary painted the donation box. Ash painted the sign.

Mary walked over to him and studied his face. "You have a bit of paint here. Let me get it." She wiped his cheek with the corner of her apron. "Oops, I didn't get it all." She gave another wipe while trying mightily to keep the smile off her face.

"Let me see your other side." She put her finger under his chin and turned his face. "You have got some there, too." She gave a couple wipes to his cheek. "That's got it. Are we done?" She was already striding up the lane. When she reached the house, she doubled over with laughter.

Naomi opened the door. "What are you cackling about?"

"I found a new friend for Weeble."

Ash came walking up. Naomi clapped her hand over her mouth to hold back her laughter.

Ash looked at them both. "What's so funny?"

Mary couldn't keep her trick a secret any longer. "You have whiskers like a kitten only they're blue."

Ash rubbed at his face, but the thin smears of paint were already dry. Naomi went in the house and returned with a hand mirror. Ash looked at himself and then at Mary. "How did I ever get the impression that you have a serious nature? What hint in your letters did I miss?"

She raised her hands in an innocent shrug. "I don't know. Maybe I'm good at pretending."

Mary was outside with Esther watching her bring a bouquet of roses to life on her sketch pad when she heard a vehicle stop at the end of the lane. She tapped Esther's shoulder to get her attention.

When Esther looked over, Mary said, "I think I hear the mail truck. I'm going to see if there is a letter for me."

"It has only been a week."

"But it's possible I could get a reply this soon. I'm going to check."

Mary hurried out the gate and ran down to the highway. The white mail truck was pulling away. She opened the mailbox. It was stuffed full.

After pulling out the bundle, she sorted through it as she walked back. Nothing for her, but there was a letter for Ash. The return address was Bird-in-Hand but no name. She carried the mail up to the house, trying not to be disappointed. Maybe tomorrow she would have an answer.

Ash was at the kitchen table with his mother and Gabe when Mary came in. He looked up and smiled, making her heart turn over with happiness. They had spent every evening together this past week, sitting in the garden, playing games with his brothers after supper, taking walks in the woods. She liked it best when they went up to the field of flowers and watched the sun go down. It was impossible to describe how happy she was. She might not remember her past, but a future with Ash was a wonderful possibility. Once she made amends.

"Anything?" he asked.

"Not for me." She didn't have to hide her disappointment. He understood all too well how important it was to her. "You have a letter from

Bird-in-Hand. The rest are bills, magazines, the *Budget* and some junk mail."

He took the letter from Mary. "Bird-in-Hand? Who do we know there, Mamm?"

"Let me think. Your cousin Jeffery lives there."

"We aren't particularly close. Wonder why he would write to me?" Ash tore open the letter, unfolded it and began to read. His eyes widened. The color left his face. Something was wrong.

"Is it from Jeffery? Is it bad news?" Talitha asked with concern.

He blinked several times as he stared at Mary. "It's not from Jeffery." He held out the page to his mother. "It's from Mary Kate Brenneman."

Mary's heart pounded in her chest as he stared at her. This couldn't be right. It was a mistake. "I didn't write it."

"How is this possible?" Talitha took the page from him.

The blank expression in his eyes terrified Mary. "She apologizes for the delay in coming to stay with us, but she'll be here the day after tomorrow." He shook his head. "How did I not know?"

"Who would play a cruel joke like this?" Gabe snatched up the letter.

Mary couldn't breathe. "It must be a prank."

Ash never took his eyes off her. "It's no joke. That's Mary Kate's handwriting."

"What does this mean?" Her voice was a bare whimper. She stepped back until she came up against the wall. The room started to spin.

Ash propped his elbows on the table and rested his head on his hands. When he looked at her, his eyes were full of sorrow. "It means there has been a terrible mistake. You're not Mary Kate Brenneman."

She stretched one hand toward him. A muffled roar filled her ears. "If I'm not Mary, who am I? Ash, who am I?"

The spinning room tilted and went black.

Chapter Twelve

When Mary opened her eyes, she was in her room on the bed. The arrival of the horrible letter and the aftermath came rushing into her mind. Bile burned the back of her throat as her stomach lurched. Why couldn't it be a bad dream? Everything she thought she knew about herself was untrue.

Talitha sat beside her and placed a cool cloth on her forehead. "You fainted. How are you feeling?"

Like she was leaning over the rim of the huge, gaping dark hole, flailing her arms to keep from plunging into the darkness forever.

"I'm fine." It was a lie, but it didn't matter. Why worry Talitha?

"Mamm, I'd like to speak to Mary alone," Ash said from the doorway.

She turned her face toward the wall. "I'm not Mary. I'm nobody."

Talitha squeezed her shoulder. "You are some-one. You're a child of *Gott*. You are special to Him. And to us. Do not forget that."

"Why? I've forgotten everything else."

"Mary, please speak to me," Ash pleaded.

She rolled away from the comfort Talitha of-fered, and the heartache Ash brought with him. "Don't call me that. Call me Jane Doe or Mary Nobody if you must call me something. I want to be alone, now."

"Very well." Talitha sighed heavily and got up from the bed. She and Ash left the room.

When Mary heard the door close, she wanted to cry, but tears didn't come. Knowing she wasn't the woman Ash had planned to marry devastated her. If there was one saving grace to the situa-tion, it was that she had never told him she loved him. Telling him now would only hurt him. That secret would be hers alone until her dying day.

What did she do now? She didn't belong with the Fishers, kind as they were. She didn't be-long to Ash.

Why had *Gott* allowed her to love him? His kiss had been so tender it made her heart ache to remember it.

She loved him. That wouldn't change because she wasn't his Mary Kate Brenneman.

A sense of calm settled over her. She sat up and wiped her face. If she loved him, she had to help him through this difficult time. She saw the pain on his face when he read the letter. He was suffering as she was. Now it was her turn to be strong. For him.

Ash paced across the kitchen and back. His brothers and his father sat quietly at the table watching him. He stopped when he heard someone coming down the stairs. His mother walked into the room. Her expression was grim.

He folded his arms tightly across his chest. "How is she?"

"Understandably upset. How could we have made such a mistake?"

He spread his hands. "How was I to know? I assumed she was Mary Kate because I was expecting Mary Kate. She had my letter in her hand."

"Perhaps she is a friend of Mary Kate's?" his mother suggested.

He pressed his palms to his temples. "I should've guessed. There were so many things about her that didn't make sense. She's not practical and serious."

She was funny, sensitive and utterly adorable. He was head over heels in love with her. And he might be engaged to the real Mary Kate Brenneman.

"What are you going to do?" Gabe asked.

"I have no idea. I'm in love with her, that much I do know. I think she loves me, too. My plan was to ask her to marry me as soon as her situation in Ohio was resolved. Only she doesn't have a situation in Ohio. There's nothing to hold her back now."

"She may already be married," Seth said.

Ash dropped onto the nearest chair with a weight like an anvil on his heart. He struggled to breathe. "You're right. Why didn't I think of that?"

She wasn't Mary Kate Brenneman from Ohio who had come to Maine to marry him. She had a family and a home somewhere. Perhaps even a husband and children. Were they searching for her, wondering why she hadn't returned or written, eaten up with worry as he would be?

He looked at the ceiling. "I should go up and try to talk to her again."

"Not yet," his mother said. "Give her a little more time to take this in. The real Mary Kate will be here tomorrow. She may have answers to all of this."

Ash bowed his head. Her letter said she had the answer to his question. His stomach roiled at the thought. Nothing good ever came of impulsive actions.

Seth got to his feet. "We promised Jesse Crump his wheel today. We should go finish it. Come on, Ash. You can't do anything here. Mamm will let us know when Mary is ready to face you. I reckon we can still call her Mary, can't we?"

"You can," she said from the doorway. "There is more than one Mary in the world. If it would make you more comfortable, call me Mary. Ash, may I speak to you alone?"

Her face was pale, but her voice was steady. He got up. "Of course. Let's go into the garden."

She flinched but nodded and smiled. It didn't reach her eyes. There was no sparkle in them when she looked at him now. Ash followed her from the room feeling the gaze of his entire family on him.

In the garden she took a seat on the bench. He stood beside her with his arms folded. "I'm sorry about this, Mary."

"It's not your fault, Ash."

"I'm the one who told you and everybody else who I thought you were."

"Because that is what you believed. Enough wallowing in pity. This has happened and we must face it. I'm not Mary Kate Brenneman. She is on her way here expecting to meet the man she has grown fond of. Now I can start a search for my true identity. Perhaps the police can aid me. People must be searching for me. I hope someone is. This is a blessing. I wasn't shunned in

Ohio but who knows, maybe I've been shunned somewhere else."

"How can you joke about this?" He sat down beside her and took her hand. "You know how I feel."

She pulled her hand away and placed her fingers on his lips. "Don't say anything. Knowing you has been wonderful. I will never forget you. Well, maybe I shouldn't promise that."

"Mary, please. I adore your quirky sense of humor but not now."

"I'm sorry. You will have a place in my heart forever, Ash. You'll get over this. In time what we had together will just be a beautiful dream."

"What do you mean?"

"I can't stay here, Ash."

"Of course you can. You're part of this family." His voice broke the way his heart was breaking.

She cupped his cheek. "I wish I could be, but I can't."

He pressed his hand over hers to hold on to her a little longer. "You're leaving? Where will you go?" He wanted her near, but he wanted her safe and happy even more. Why was God doing this to them?

"Naomi will take me in. With her help I can start searching for the place I belong."

"You belong with us." Tears welled up in his eyes. "With me," he wanted to shout but that wasn't possible unless Mary Kate was coming to refuse him. He prayed that would happen even as he accepted it was unlikely.

He had asked her to marry him, and he knew the honorable thing to do. If she accepted, he would be true to her no matter the cost to his heart. And the price would be high.

Mary's lip quivered. "Please, let me go. I have to find answers."

He sniffed and wiped his cheeks. "I want you to find them, but I don't want to lose my best friend."

"You won't," she said softly. "This isn't about you and me anymore. You have been part of Mary Kate's life much longer than you have known me. You had a connection that reached across a thousand miles before we even met. Don't discard what the two of you had because you and I were forced together by circumstances. Promise me you will give her a chance."

"I promise." He could feel his hope and happiness draining away. If he lost Mary, he would be an empty shell.

He gripped her hand between his. "Stay until Mary Kate gets here. She might have all the answers you need. You had her letter. She must have given it to you. Stay until then."

She might not want to marry me.

He didn't say the words aloud. He couldn't

bear to give Mary false hope. If all he was given was one more day with her, he would cherish it.

Mary pulled her fingers away from Ash's hand. Lingering would only make her departure that much harder, but he was right. The real Mary Kate could have the answers she needed.

"I'll stay until she arrives. We should go in now. I want to tell the others what I've decided."

Sighing, he got to his feet and held out his hand for her. She didn't take it. If he touched her again, she would break down. This was worse than waking up in the hospital and finding everything was missing. Her old life was still a blank. The problem was she had started a new one with new friends and a new family. A new love. Now she was losing it all.

Inside, the family was waiting in the living room. They could've been gathered for a funeral by the looks on their faces.

"What will you do now, Mary?" Esther asked.

"Ash and I have talked it over. The best course seems to be waiting to find out what the real Mary Kate knows about me."

"You're the real Mary," Moses said. "She's the other one."

"After I speak to her, I'll be moving in with Naomi Walker. I know she'll have me."

"You should stay with us," Zeke said. Talitha patted his arm and nodded.

"There is an extra bed in your room," Pamela said.

Mary shared a sad smile with the family. "I don't think we'd be comfortable even if it turns out that I'm her sister or her best friend." She looked at Ash. "At least not for a while."

Moses walked across the room and enveloped her in an unexpected hug. "I'm gonna miss you."

She hugged him back. "I'll miss you, too."

"Mary isn't leaving yet," Ash declared loudly. Her heart broke into a hundred pieces at the pain in his eyes. If only she could fly into his arms and tell him everything was going to be okay.

But it wasn't.

"That's right." Talitha surged to her feet. "This will all work out as our Lord intends. We must be open to His will in all things and have faith in His mercy."

The Lord was challenging her mightily. Mary prayed she could survive the trial.

She didn't sleep at all that night. It was a little after four in the morning when she gave up trying and went down to the kitchen.

Her heart leaped when she saw Ash sitting at the table, but then it plummeted. His smile turned sad, and he looked away. "You can't sleep either."

She got a glass of water and sat at the table across from him. "The waiting is always the hardest part."

"I wish things were different."

"Don't say it, Ash. It's difficult enough. Let's just get through the day. What time will the bus arrive?"

"It should stop outside New Covenant about eight o'clock. It's raining outside. Would you like to take a walk? I know you enjoy walks in the rain. You love trees and squirrels. I've seldom seen you being sensible. See, I know a lot of things about you. I just don't know why we can't be together."

"We will know the answer in *Gott's* own time, Ash. Don't torment yourself."

"That's about as easy as not trying to make yourself remember. Did that work out for you?"

She had to change the subject. "Since I'm up I may as well start breakfast for everyone and give your mother a break."

"Sure. I'll go start with the chores. Bessie will be surprised to be milked this early, but I'm sure she'll cooperate. I'll get the eggs too, so you don't have to go out in the rain." He got up, put on his hat, slipped into a raincoat and went out the door.

Mary laid her head on her arms. "Why, *Gott*? This is so unfair."

No answer came to her. She rose and went to

start on breakfast. Ash soon brought the eggs and milk in and left again. She was setting the table when the rest of the family came in. Esther and Pamela walked to her and put their arms around her. They didn't say anything, they simply held her, and she loved them for it.

Talitha went to the sink to look out the window. "Has Ash left yet?"

Mary wiped her eyes. "Not yet."

"Are you sure you want to go with him to meet the bus?"

She nodded. "The real Mary Kate may know who I am. I need to see her."

"The other Mary," Moses said.

Talitha lowered the window curtain. "It has stopped raining. Ash is hitching the buggy now."

"*Danki.* You have all been so kind to me. I'm sorry I'm not who you hoped I was."

"We pray you find all your answers today," Zeke said.

"So do I." Mary walked outside and saw Ash backing Dottie up to the buggy. He caught sight of her and stopped what he was doing. They stared at each other without speaking.

She looked down and waited. He finished hitching the mare and led her over. "I don't know what to say except that I'm sorry."

She was able to look at him then. "You have nothing to be sorry for, Ash. You have treated me with kindness and respect. I will treasure our friendship forever."

"You're more than my friend."

"I might be your married friend. Because I can't remember my vows doesn't mean I can brush them aside."

"I understand."

She didn't think she had any more tears left, but they welled up in her eyes. "You have to give Mary Kate a chance. She's come all this way. You were expecting a woman who seemed to be your perfect match. Maybe she still is."

Suddenly Mary didn't want to see their meeting. She couldn't bear knowing he belonged to another. "I've changed my mind. I'm not coming with you. The two of you need to meet without an onlooker. I'll speak to her when you bring her home."

"Are you sure?"

"I am. Don't keep her waiting." She spun away and ran around the side of the house to the garden at the back.

Ash reached the bus stop when it was still empty. He remembered the day he should have been at this place when Mary arrived. If only he had been.

The bus pulled in a few minutes later. A single Amish woman in a dark blue dress got off the bus. She was tall and sturdy looking with dark hair. She wore glasses and held a pair of suitcases. She spied him and immediately walked toward him. "Good day. Are you Asher Fisher?"

He nodded. "Are you Mary Kate Brenneman?"

"Indeed I am Mary Kate. I'm so pleased to meet you at last, Asher. You are exactly as I had pictured you from your lovely letters. I hope Mari explained everything, and you can forgive me for my delay. It was such an amazing blessing that she was on her way to Fort Craig, too. The Lord certainly put her in the right place at the right time for me."

"Mari? Her name is Mari?" He knew that much about her. She was going to be so happy.

Mary Kate scowled at him. "She called herself Mari Kemp. She did meet you and give you my message, didn't she?"

"I'm afraid things didn't go as planned. I'll tell you on the way to my home."

He explained what had happened as he drove toward the farm. Mary Kate was understandably upset by the events.

"And she has no memory of meeting me?"

"She remembers almost nothing before waking up in the hospital. The police found one of my letters in her hand at the accident. I was expecting you. I gave them your name. We all thought she was you."

"How horrible for the poor woman."

After that Ash couldn't think of a single thing to say to her. All he wanted was to see his Mary. His Mari.

"When I met my dear cousin so unexpectedly, I couldn't simply leave," Mary Kate said, her words running into each other in a rush. "We hadn't seen each other for eleven years and we were once so close. When Mari offered to explain the situation to you, I thought a few days delay coming here wouldn't make a difference. I knew you would understand. I didn't mean to linger so long with my cousin, but our visit was something I badly needed. The truth is, I was having second thoughts about coming here."

"You were?" His hopes rose. Maybe she had come to refuse him.

"In spite of my cousin's objections I realized this was the right thing to do." She turned in the seat to stare at him. "You haven't asked me what my answer is."

He knew what she was talking about. "I haven't forgotten about it."

"I certainly haven't, either. I've been giving it a great deal of thought and my answer is yes. Asher Fisher, I will marry you."

His heart dropped to his boots as his final hope died a painful death. "Don't you want some time to think it over? Don't you feel we should get to know each other better?"

"I feel I know you very well. We've been writing to each other for months. We have the same likes and dislikes. We're both practical people. I don't see any reason why this won't be a happy union."

Except that he was in love with another woman. "Do you know if Mari is married or engaged?"

"I have no idea. It didn't come up in our conversation. She did say she was coming here to find her grandmother, but she didn't mention a husband. Her poor family must be frantic after all this time."

"We contacted your family thinking they needed to know about your accident."

She made a sour face. "Oh dear. I'm sure you were shocked by what they said about me."

"I was."

"I can explain everything. It's not how they would've made it sound."

"I'm listening."

"Our bishop is my mother-in-law's brother. My in-laws and the bishop invested money in my husband's company when he was getting started. It became a wonderful success for a time. He paid them back every cent. Then the business started losing money. After he died, they claimed they each owned one third of the business and wanted to buy my third for a pittance. I refused and tried to run it myself but eventually I chose a more practical solution. I sold the entire company to one of my husband's *Englisch* friends."

Ash wasn't sure what to say. Silence seemed the best choice.

She drew a deep breath. "My in-laws were furious. They convinced people I had cheated them. I didn't, but none of the people in the community approved of my selling the company to an outsider instead of Ed's family. I regret that our family quarrel went so far. There were other problems, too, which I will tell you about later. Anyway, the Bann will be lifted if I admit I was wrong and share what I received for the business. I don't believe I was wrong, so I chose to leave." She clutched the strap of her purse tightly. "I have more to tell you, but perhaps it should wait."

They had arrived at the house. Ash stopped the buggy. Jedidiah Zook was standing by the front porch with Moses. One more problem to face.

"Asher, Moses says my wheel isn't done. You promised it would be ready today."

"We'll get it finished and deliver it to you. I'm sorry for the delay. I had to meet the bus. We have a visitor." Ash wasn't about to explain why he had another Mary Kate Brenneman staying with him.

Jedidiah tipped his hat and smiled. An unusual sight. Mary Kate smiled and nodded to him. She glanced around the property. "What a pleasant home you have, Asher, although you might want to think about cutting back some of the forest. Those trees rather overwhelm the place."

"I've told Zeke Fisher that a dozen times," Jedidiah said.

Ash bristled. "I like the trees. I like all the trees just as they are."

Her eyes widened at his tone. "I'm sure the woods have many practical uses."

"The squirrels live there. They like their homes. I said I'd bring your wheel by later, Jed." Ash glared at him, got out of the buggy and helped Mary Kate down. Jedidiah strolled away, got in his buggy and drove off.

Ash reined in his temper. He never got this upset. "Mary, I mean Mari, is anxious to meet you. You are the one person who knows her. Please treat her gently. She has had a difficult time."

"Of course. Where can I find her?"

His mother came out of the house. Ash made the introductions. "Our Mary's name is Mari Kemp. Where is she?"

"She's in the garden. Ash, why don't you show Mrs. Brenneman the way."

* * *

Mary heard the door to the house open. She looked over and saw an Amish woman come into the garden. Tall and muscular, she moved with confidence as she approached. She sat on the bench. "Mari, you poor thing. Asher told me what happened."

Mary blinked hard. "What did you call me?"

"Mari. Your name is Mari Kemp."

She sucked in a breath. "I'm Mari Kemp, not Mary Kate. No wonder my name sounded only half right."

"All this time people thought you were me?"

Excitement poured through Mari's veins as pieces of her life popped into her head. "We were on the same bus. I remember. You were coming here, but you met someone while we were waiting to change buses."

"My cousin Sarah. I hadn't seen her in years."

"I said I would let Ash know why you weren't at the bus stop to meet him."

"You were searching for your grandmother near Fort Craig. Did you find her?"

Mari jumped to her feet. "Naomi Helmuth. I think I've met her, but her name is Walker now. Tell me where I'm from."

"Arthur, Illinois, I believe."

Mari paced back and forth. "I'm Mari Kemp. I'm twenty-three years old not twenty-nine. I'm from Arthur. There's nothing but cornfields for miles around our home."

A new memory struck her. She sat down, overcome with sadness. "My *daed* died three months ago. He drowned trying to rescue another man during a flash flood. Oh, Papa!" She doubled over in pain. It was the one memory she didn't want back.

Mary Kate laid a hand on Mari's arm. "I'm sorry to hear that."

Drawing a shaky breath, Mari sat up. "It was a shock when I found letters he'd written to his mother. They had all been returned unopened. I was alone in the world. I have no other family. I needed to find her. That's why I came."

She threw her arm around Mary Kate and hugged her. "I remember. Thank you so much."

When Mari opened her eyes, she saw Ash watching them from the doorway. Her heart sank. She wasn't married, but she remembered now why Mary Kate had come to Maine. The reason she needed to marry Ash.

He was too far away to overhear them. Mari sat back and braced herself to learn Mary Kate's decision. "Since you're here, I assume your reason for coming hasn't changed."

"It hasn't. I see no other choice. I spoke to the only friend I still have back home. She said my son Matthew cries for me all the time. We need to be together. I'll do anything to make that happen. I have accepted Asher's proposal of marriage."

"Do you care for Ash at all, or is he a means to an end?"

A soft smile transformed Mary Kate's face. "Asher's letters drew me out of a dark place. He wrote about his home and the wonderful people of this community, about his dreams and what he wanted his future to look like. His sensitive, caring letters made me believe that I could start over here."

"Have you told Ash about your son?"

She looked down. "Not yet. When we first started writing, I couldn't bring myself to share how I failed Matthew after my husband died. What mother wants to admit she couldn't take care of her own child? I was ashamed of myself. The troubles with my in-laws made it worse. I didn't want to burden him with the sordid details."

"He would have understood," Mari said.

"I know, but when I read Asher's letters, I could forget my own problems. After the bishop said I had to marry to get Matthew back, I was afraid Asher would stop writing if he knew the whole truth about what a mess I had made of my life. Then he proposed marriage in his last letter, and I saw a way out. I thought if I told him everything in person, I could make him understand.

I'll tell him everything today. I pray he can forgive my omission and help me get my son back."

Mari faced the hardest choice of her life. If she told Mary Kate that she was in love with Ash she would ruin two lives by keeping a mother from her son. If she remained silent and left, Ash would gain a wife and a son the way he would have if her accident hadn't happened. If she'd simply given him the message and then gone on to look for Naomi.

He'd be a good father to a sad little boy.

"Ash loves children. He's a wonderful man, my best friend. We became very close. You must tell him the whole truth. It won't be easy for him to hear. He'll need time to adjust. Can you give him that time?"

Mary Kate gripped Mari's hand. "Of course I will. I'm so sorry this happened."

Mari gazed at Ash's troubled face where he stood by the house. "*Gott* allowed it. We trust it is part of His plan."

She walked toward Ash to say goodbye to her heart.

Chapter Thirteen

Mari Kemp. How long would it take him to get used to her name? How much time did he have? Was she about to vanish from his life? As she walked toward him, he knew she had the answers she had sought for so long.

When she stopped in front of him, the sadness in her eyes matched what was in his heart. "You remember."

"I do. Everything."

The lump lodged in his throat made him swallow hard. "And?"

"I'll be leaving today."

How could those simple words hurt so much? He closed his eyes and tipped his head back as the pain engulfed him. This wasn't happening.

"I'm sorry, Ash. My home is in Arthur, Illinois. I came here searching for my grandmother, Naomi Helmuth. I'm sure she's Naomi Walker.

That's the reason she seemed familiar. My father looked so much like her. Their eyes are exactly the same. They were estranged before I was born. That's why she didn't recognize me. I'm told I take after my mother, and they never met. I plan to spend a few days getting better acquainted with her."

He knew the answer, but he had to ask. "Was there any chance for us?"

She looked down. "*Nee*. Mary Kate has some things she'd like to tell you."

He clenched his fingers into fists. "What's his name? The reason we couldn't be together?"

Mari laid her palm against his cheek. He'd never forget the feel of her small soft hands on his skin.

"It doesn't matter, Ash."

"I want to know."

She glanced over her shoulder at Mary Kate and then looked into his eyes. "Matthew."

So she had a husband, or she was promised as he was. Ash struggled to speak. "He's blessed. I hope he knows that."

A sad smile pulled at the corner of her mouth. "Dear Ash, I'm going to miss you so much. I can never repay what you and your family have done for me. I'll keep you and Mary Kate in my prayers every night of my life. Goodbye, Asher Ethan Fisher."

Tears filled his eyes and ran down his face. "Goodbye, Mari Kemp."

He couldn't bear it any longer. He turned and went into the house so he didn't have to watch her walk away from him.

Talitha, Esther and Pamela came out. Talitha wrapped her arms around Mari. "Our hearts are broken."

"Time will mend them." Mari didn't believe it. Her heart would never be whole, but she wanted to give these wonderful women some comfort.

"What can we do?" Pamela asked.

"Be kind to Mary Kate. She needs your help and support. Take care of Ash. I know he's hurting."

"You are, too," Talitha said.

"But I have my life back. All of it. From the window I broke at school during recess in the first grade, to sneaking out to see a movie during my *rumspringa*, to my father's tragic death. I'm going to see Naomi now. I'm sure she is my grandmother. I'll let you know where to send my things. Thank you for everything. I shouldn't say this, but I'll never forget you."

No one chuckled as she had hoped. Turning away, Mari hurried to the garden gate and let herself out. Running through the woods was awkward with her cast. She tried to outdistance her heartache but couldn't leave it behind. At the highway she slowed to a walk. She had done the right thing for everyone. That was what she needed to remember, not the look of pain on Ash's face.

It took her half an hour to reach Naomi's lane. She paused at the freshly painted sign for Walker Animal Sanctuary. She and Ash had painted it together. There would be reminders of their time together everywhere. As much as she wanted to stay in New Covenant, she realized it wouldn't be possible. To stay would mean seeing Ash and Mary Kate together.

She would go home and take up her life. Maybe she could get her old job back in the fabric shop where she had worked before her father's death. She wouldn't be alone anymore. She had a grandmother, even if she did live in Maine.

She didn't see Naomi in the yard or the pens. She walked up to the front door and knocked.

The door opened and Naomi stood there with flour on her shirt and arms. "Mary Kate, I wasn't expecting you today."

"My real name is Mari Kemp. I think you are my *grossmammi*."

Naomi grew deathly pale and pressed a hand to her chest. "You're mistaken."

Disappointment snatched Mari's breath away. She couldn't be wrong.

"You should leave now." Naomi tried to shut the door.

Why was Naomi, her friend, shutting her out?

Realization dawned. Because it was true. Mari stood her ground. "You knew who I was, didn't you?"

"I have no idea what you're talking about." She pushed on the door, but Mari pushed back.

"My father was Gerald Kemp. He was estranged from his mother. I thought she was dead, but when my father passed away, I found a bundle of letters tied up with a blue ribbon. They were all addressed to Naomi Helmuth. Twenty-three letters. Postmarked on my birthday every year and every one of them was returned unopened. Letters addressed to Africa, the Dominican Republic, other far-away places."

"Please stop." Naomi retreated into her kitchen.

Mari followed her. "I read them. They all started with the same sentence. 'My dearest mother, I forgive you.'"

Naomi braced her hands on the counter and bowed her head. "I don't know how he could."

"Did you know about me? Did you know you abandoned a son and a grandchild?"

Naomi shook her head. "I knew he married. I didn't know about you until I read his obituary. I still take the Amish newspaper."

"Why did you return all his letters? That was so cruel."

"I wanted him to forget about me. I was never coming back. He had to accept that."

Mari gaped at her in disbelief. "He didn't forget you, but he never said a word about you. Why did you leave?"

"It's a long story. I can't bear to tell it."

"I'm not leaving until I understand."

"Oh, very well." Naomi turned around. "I was widowed when your father was five. I raised him alone until I met a wonderful man and fell deeply in love. We married when your father was fifteen. It wasn't what I had hoped for."

"In what way?"

"He and Isaac didn't get along. They quarreled often. Isaac felt strongly that God was calling him to the ministry. The Amish don't believe in such callings. Our bishop said Isaac was prideful for claiming God wanted him to become a preacher. After three horrible years of disagreements, Isaac was shunned because he wouldn't deny his belief."

Mari sat down at the table. "What happened?"

Naomi remained at the counter. "Isaac chose to join another faith, enter their ministry and become a missionary. I had a choice. Remain Amish or be shunned with my husband. I chose to go with Isaac. That meant turning my back on my friends, my vows to the church and it meant leaving your father. He was only eighteen. It was the hardest choice I ever had to make."

"Did you regret it?"

"That's a foolish question."

"I'm sorry." What choice could Naomi have made without regrets? What choice could Mari have made without regrets? "You must have loved your husband very much."

"Oh, I did. He was an amazing human being.

"Your father was forbidden to have any contact with me. If I had answered his letters, I would have risked him being shunned, too. I knew what the Amish faith meant to my son. I'm ashamed to learn my silence harmed him just as much."

"He forgave you."

"Hearing those words from you eases the ache that has never left my soul."

"How is it that your name is Walker now?"

"After we left Illinois, I went to school and became a nurse. Isaac and I worked together in Africa and at other missions for fifteen wonderful years. He died in Haiti. I was lost without him and lonely. I married again a few years later, but it didn't work out. He left me. I withdrew from the world after that. I was tired of being hurt. That's when I started taking care of injured animals. I found comfort in helping wild creatures and eventually I found healing. And then a little fox brought my granddaughter into my life in a most unexpected fashion."

Mari smiled. "*Gott* moves in mysterious ways."

"That He does. I'm thankful your memory has returned. How did that happen?"

"The real Mary Kate walked into the garden this morning and called me Mari. It was like a dam burst. Memories came flooding back so quickly it was hard to take them in. Then I remembered why I was coming to Fort Craig. To find you and get answers."

"I didn't know who you were when we first met. I only knew that you reminded me of my son. You have his smile and his ears."

"He had your eyes. The first time I looked at you, I had a vision of him. That's what made me faint. I think the pain I experienced was grief."

"You must miss him."

"I treasure every memory I have of him."

"I imagine Ash is thrilled for you."

Mari looked away. "He proposed to Mary Kate in one of his letters. She has accepted him. Things will go back to the way they should be if I'm not here."

"I'm so sorry. You love him, don't you?"

Mari's throat tightened. "I do. Ever since the day I opened my eyes in the hospital, and he became my whole world."

"What are you going to do now?"

"I'll go back to Arthur."

Naomi slipped her arm around Mari's shoulders. "I have room for one more in my collection of injured souls."

Mari sniffled. "Are you offering me a place to stay?"

"I understand if you would rather not. You know, because I left the Amish, and all."

Mari grasped Naomi's hand and squeezed. "My father forgave you. I would not be his daughter if I did any less. I'd love to stay with you for a few days."

"Even if I've been shunned? I belonged to your church district."

"We will work around it. We can't eat at the same table."

"I'll eat at the counter," Naomi said quickly.

Mari grinned. "Or I can. I can't do business with you so you can't pay me to work here. I can't ride in your truck, so you'll have to find someone else to take me to the bus station."

"Not too soon, I pray."

"This is the hard one. I can't accept anything from your hand. Not a fork, not animal feed, not a glass of water."

"I know. I must leave things so that you can pick them up yourself. There are no rules that say I can't hug you." She enfolded Mari and pulled her close.

This was what Mari had dreamed of finding. A loving grandmother. After a minute, she drew back. "You can always join a more progressive Amish church like the one here. That way your shunning in Arthur won't matter anymore."

"I'll think about it. I do miss worshiping with others. Bless you, child. Your kindness means the world to me. You can call me grandma if you want."

"I'd like that."

Naomi cleared her throat. "Since you're here, the animals in the barn need feeding and those miserable geese are out again."

"It will help to stay busy until I can get a bus ticket back to Arthur, but I can't stay long."

"I understand and I'm sorry. Trouble is doing well enough to be released in a few days. I hope you'll stay until then."

"I can do that." As long as she didn't have to see Ash.

Ash was stunned by what Mary Kate revealed to him in the garden that evening. She had a child she had failed to mention. Tearfully, she recounted the circumstances that led to her coming to Maine. He didn't know any Amish family as unkind to one another as hers had been. It wasn't the way a child should be raised.

"I'm deeply sorry for my deception. I grew to care for you when we wrote to each other. Please believe that part was true."

It was a lot to take in, but he heard the sincerity in her voice. "I do believe you, and I forgive you. A mother should have her child with her."

She smiled with relief. "Mari said you were a good man, that you would understand." Her smile faded. "If you don't wish to marry me, I will accept that."

Mari thought he was a good man. He wasn't. He was a hurt, angry, sad man. She had walked away from him because somewhere in her life was a man named Matthew. If he couldn't marry the woman he loved, then maybe he should help this woman who loved her son. "I haven't changed my mind."

"Are you sure? Mari said you would need time to think things over. She knew this would be difficult for you. I'm glad the two of you became friends. She's a very sensible woman."

"Actually, she isn't."

Ash left Mary Kate and spent the rest of the evening counting and recounting the bolts, springs, door handles and washers in the shop. He wasn't surprised when Gabe and Seth came in. They went to the bins and each opened a drawer.

"Ten left rear turn signals." Gabe closed his bin.

"Eight headlamps." Seth looked at Ash. "Did you get that?"

"You don't need to try to cheer me up. I'm doing okay."

His brothers looked at each other and chuckled. "Doing inventory cheers him up," Gabe said with a grin.

Seth pulled open another drawer. "This one is empty. We're missing one sweet, funny, impractical girl with her arm in a cast. What shall we do?"

Ash put his ledger down. "She's irreplaceable but unavailable."

"We're sorry, Ash," Gabe said. "What are you going to do?"

"Make the best of it. I'll gain a son and a wife."

Seth frowned. "You can't be serious."

Ash just wanted to be alone. "Go back in the house."

Gabe nodded toward the door. "Jedidiah Zook is here for a visit again. His girls were disappointed to miss Mary."

"Mari," Ash said through tight lips.

Gabe nodded. "They seem to like the other Mary Kate well enough. She's teaching them to play Settlers of Catan with Moses and Jed. You didn't mention she had a son before this, Ash. Apparently, it's his favorite game. She teared up when she said it. What's going on?"

Ash drew a deep breath. "I reckon she misses her boy."

"Jed was winning. We're not going back inside," Seth stated firmly.

Ash almost smiled. "Thanks for the warning."

Gabe opened the next bin. "Eight right rear turn signals."

"I think I'll go in and join the game." Ash handed his ledger to Seth. Mari was out of reach. Accepting that was hard. He should at least get to know the real Mary Kate before they chose a wedding date.

Mari snuggled Weeble against her face and listened to the kitten's loud purring. She was always a happy little thing. Mari wished she could follow Weeble's lead. Waiting on Naomi to return with her clothing and things had Mari on edge. Would Naomi see Ash? Would he ask about her? Was Mary Kate settling in?

The battered brown pickup came rumbling down the drive. Placing Weeble gently on the floor, Mari then dashed out the door. When she reached the truck, she pulled open Naomi's door. "Did you see him? How is he?"

"I saw him all right. He's busy creating a storm in that family. Everyone is in an uproar."

"What do you mean?"

"He and the new Mary Kate are going to see the bishop tomorrow about setting a date for their wedding. Why is he jumping into a huge mistake so fast? I thought the man had more sense."

"He's actually going to marry her?" Deep in her heart, Mari had secretly cherished the hope that it wouldn't happen.

She had encouraged the relationship, but now she wished she had kept silent. When he married, he would truly be lost to her forever. "They've known each other a long time."

"That may be, but the boy is in love with you! He's not being fair to that woman."

"She needs a husband."

"What she deserves is a man who loves her beyond all reason. A marriage based on anything less will struggle to survive."

"The Amish do not allow divorce."

"I'm not talking about splitting up. I'm talking about sharing hopes, dreams and sorrows with someone who understands and respects you. When that dies, a couple can stay together but the true marriage is dead. Then two people spend their lives in misery."

"That's not going to happen to Ash. He'll

fall in love with Mary Kate again. He did once before."

"I pray you are right. His mother and brothers sure don't think so."

"Talitha can be wrong."

"We all can. I'm taking Trouble's splint off today. If he gets around fine without it, we can release him back into the wild tomorrow."

"That will be wonderful. Then can you arrange for someone to take me to the bus station?"

"No."

Mari frowned. "Why not?"

"Because you'd be jumping into a mistake, too. Why did Ash stop seeing you?"

"Because of Matthew."

"Who is Matthew?"

"He's the reason Ash and I can't be together."

"Are you promised to him?"

"*Nee*. I'll find someone who can take me to the bus, or I can walk."

"I read my son's obituary. It listed his daughter by her maiden name. No mention of a husband. Whoever Matthew is, he doesn't have a claim on you. Stubborn runs in your family, child. I should know. Don't let it ruin your life."

Tears gathered in Mari's eyes. "It's too late." She turned and ran into the house.

Naomi planted her hands on her hips. "Not while your grandmother is still breathing."

* * *

Ash went to hitch up the buggy after breakfast the next day and found a note on the seat with his name on it. Was it from Mari? He tore it open. The fine penmanship canceled that hope.

Ash, she isn't married. She isn't engaged. She loves you.

Would you want Mari married to someone who doesn't love her?

Do the right thing. Tell Mary Kate you're in love with Mari. Let her make the choice.

It wasn't signed, but he suspected Naomi was the author.

Would you want Mari married to someone who doesn't love her?

Never. Mari deserved so much better.

"I'm ready to go, Ash," Mary Kate said behind him.

He turned around and looked at the woman waiting for him. And so did she.

"Mary Kate, I have something important I need to say to you."

"If you're upset that Jedidiah Zook asked me to walk out with him, he didn't know about our engagement. I refused him, of course without giving a reason. I thought he should learn about it the same time as the rest of the community when our bans are announced in church."

"It's not that."

"Okay." She waited with a curious expression in her eyes.

"First you should know that I intend to marry you and reunite you with your son."

"That's reassuring."

"But you need to know that I'm in love with someone else."

Her eyes widened. "What did you just say?"

"I'm in love with Mari."

Mary Kate rocked back. "Well finally. I didn't think you were ever going to admit it."

"You mean you knew?"

"I strongly suspected. I watched the two of you together, trying desperately not to fall into each other's arms the first day I arrived. I felt sorry for the two of you, but I thought if it was true love, you wouldn't go ahead with our engagement. Now that I know the truth, I won't marry you. I hope you have told the poor girl how you feel."

"Actually, I haven't. I am engaged to you. Is our engagement off?"

"I suppose it is." Her eyes grew serious. "Do you truly love her, Ash?"

"More than my own life."

She blinked back tears. "Then I'm doing the right thing."

"Would you have married me suspecting that I love her?"

She tipped her head as she regarded him. "Love is a strange gift the Lord has given us. It expands as we use it. We love our parents when we are young. I love my son more than I can say. If we are blessed, we love our spouses.

"I loved my husband deeply. I never expected to feel that way about any man again. I thought I would be content with someone I liked and respected, who liked and respected me in turn. I would've tried to be a good wife to you, Ash. I suspect you would have tried to be a good husband to me. Thankfully, now neither of us has to try. It seems love is expanding again. I suggest you go find Mari and tell her how much she means to you. That kind of love should be cherished."

"But what about you and your son?"

"I will find a way to reunite with Matthew. I won't ever give up."

"Your son's name is Matthew?" he asked in surprise.

"It is. Didn't I mention that?"

"*Nee,* but Mari did." The name of the reason they couldn't be together. "You should walk out with Jedidiah if he asks you again."

She laughed. "I don't think that will take much encouragement on my part. I do kind of fancy him. He has the most amazing brown eyes and he's trying hard to be father to those adorable girls. I like him."

"He also has the largest farm out of all the Amish in the district."

"I suspected he had more good qualities. He needs some adjustments, but he may do."

"I wish you the very best, Mary Kate. If not for you I would have never met Mari." He bent and kissed her cheek.

"Finding a deep and abiding love is a great treasure, Ash. Never squander it, never hoard it. Give it freely and it will come back to you tenfold. I had it once. I would never take it away from someone else. I'm glad you said something before it was too late. Now go. I'm sure Mari is quite miserable believing that she is losing you forever."

He didn't need further urging. He hurried to the corral and harnessed Frisky to the buggy and drove out of the yard. He kept her to her fastest pace until he pulled up in front of Naomi Walker's front porch.

He jumped out and ran up the steps. Naomi was coming out the door just as he reached it. "I see you got my note."

"I have to see Mari. Where is she?"

"She's taking the little fox out to be released."

"Where?"

"Near where you found the den."

"Great. I know right where that is. *Danki*, for all you've done for her."

"She has done much more for me. I'm almost sorry to lose her to you."

He smiled. "You aren't losing her. I'll make sure of that." He jogged away from the house along the path that led to the pond where he had first kissed his Mary Kate. His Mari.

When he reached the clearing, he stopped. She was on her knees in the grass beside a pink dog crate. He could see that she was crying.

"I'm going to miss you, Trouble. But this is where you belong. You must promise to stay off the highway. Are you ready? I should be happy for you, my friend, but I'm not." She opened the cage door. The kit ran out and headed for the den. At the shrubbery, he stopped, looked back and made a series of clucking sounds before disappearing inside.

Ash walked up beside her. "That's the sound a fox makes greeting a friend. I'm glad I got to see that."

She wiped her eyes with the back of her hand and stood up. "I know what it is. What are you doing here? I thought you and Mary Kate had an appointment to see the bishop about the wedding date."

"We did, but the wedding is off so there's no

point in going to see him. Are you ready to go back?"

Her eyes grew wide. "What did you just say?"

"Are you ready to go back?"

"You are a maddening man. Before that."

"You mean the part about the wedding being off?"

"Why? Mary Kate is perfect for you. She's practical and realistic and she doesn't rescue injured wild animals."

"Exactly." He stepped closer, wanting to pull her into his arms and hold her for a lifetime.

She took a step back. "I don't understand."

"It's simple, really. I'm not in love with Mary Kate. I'm head over heels in love with an impractical, funny, charming, adorable woman who likes to rescue injured animals and a stuffy fellow who didn't know he needed rescuing until she came into his life. Mary Kate has wisely chosen not to marry a man who is in love with someone else."

Her face lit up with the most amazing smile he had ever seen. "She has? You are?"

"I absolutely am in love with you. The only question I have is do you love me just a little?"

"No."

He drew back. "What?"

She threw her arms around his neck. "I don't love you just a little—I love you more than I can ever say. But perhaps I can show you." She rose on tiptoe and pressed her lips to his.

Ash's heart soared with joy as he gathered her close. He hadn't known it was possible to be so happy.

Mari drew back and gazed at the man she loved, unable to grasp how her despair had turned into exhilaration in a matter of minutes. "I can't believe it. I thought I'd lost you forever."

He pulled her close and tucked her head under his chin. "I almost allowed that to happen."

"Is Mary Kate heartbroken?" Mari hated that her joy came at the price of someone else's pain.

"She isn't. She suspected that I was in love with you, and yet she was going to marry me."

"She was doing it for her son. A mother's love knows no bounds. Now what will she do?"

"Jedidiah Zook asked her to walk out with him yesterday. She told him no because we were engaged but now we're not. She likes the guy and his nieces."

Mari was skeptical. "She likes Jedidiah Zook?"

"Apparently, he has the most amazing brown eyes, and an exceptionally large farm. If it is meant to be, it will work out. Look at us. *Gott* in His wisdom brought us together."

"I understand the attraction of brown eyes with thick dark lashes. I also love brown hair that curls over my fingers when I slip my hands through it like this." She proceeded to toss his hat aside and run her fingers through his hair.

He gave a low growl and pulled her close. She winced. He was instantly contrite. "Oh, Mari, I'm sorry. Did I hurt you?"

"My rib is still tender. But my face doesn't hurt."

He latched his hands behind her back but left a little distance between them. "It doesn't hurt here anymore?" He kissed her forehead.

"Not a bit."

"What about here?" He brushed his lips across her temple. A shiver ran down her spine.

"Didn't feel a thing." Did she sound breathless? Her heart was galloping.

"This spot still has a fading bruise." He kissed her cheekbone. "Is it sore?"

"A little, but my lips aren't." She licked them and pressed them together.

"I wouldn't want to neglect your lips if they don't ache."

"Please don't neglect them, Ash."

He chuckled. "I love you."

"I'm sorry I didn't quite hear that."

"*Ja*, you did."

"How do you know?" she snapped back.

"By the sparkle in your eyes when you look at me."

"Oh, that gave me away, did it? My lips are still waiting, darling."

"I haven't forgotten." He settled his mouth over hers tenderly. The warmth of his touch flooded her heart with delight.

He lifted his head to gaze at her. "I can't believe I almost let you walk out of my life."

"It was more my fault than yours."

"That's true. You have to make it up to me."

"I can do that." She grabbed a handful of his hair and pulled his head down so she could kiss him. And keep on kissing him. Because nothing mattered but proving she loved him with all her might.

The uncertain path God had set before her brought her to the place where her heart belonged. She would never forget to give thanks for His amazing blessing.

Epilogue

Ash clenched and opened his icy fingers as his three brothers inspected him from all angles, smoothed his vest across his chest and brushed imaginary lint from the shoulders of his black *mutza* suit. He wasn't exactly sure how he'd gotten himself into this situation.

That wasn't true. God's plan, roundabout as it may have seemed, had brought him to this point.

Gabe took a step back. "You'll do."

Moses lifted Ash's black hat from the pegs by the door. "You're not nervous, are you?"

"Of course he is," Seth declared. "He's about to get married. He's bound to be nervous."

Ash snatched his hat from his little brother's hands. "I'm not nervous. I'm on my way to wed the most amazing woman who for some reason believes she is in love with me."

He jammed his hat on his head. What if Mari

had changed her mind? What if he wasn't a good enough husband for her?

Those around him smothered their chuckles. He glanced up at his brim and turned his hat the right way around.

"He's lying," Seth said.

Gabe nodded. "He's scared to death."

"Being the most sensible brother should entitle me to a little more respect," Ash said. His brothers laughed.

"You mean most stodgy." Gabe straightened Ash's bow tie, the one an Amish fellow only wore on his wedding day.

"He's the dull one, all right. She could do better." Seth shook his head sadly.

"Dull as ditchwater," Moses added with a chuckle. "But she couldn't do better. I hope Mari knows how fortunate she is."

Ash glanced at his brothers' faces. "She could do better, but no man could love her more. I will do everything in my power to make her happy."

He gazed out the front door standing open to a beautiful fall morning and took a deep breath allowing his heart to expand with pent-up joy. His bride was waiting for him at her grandmother's house.

Outside, Jedidiah Zook stood at the door of the buggy Ash's brothers had washed and shined until it gleamed. A young boy in a dark suit and hat stood at his side. Ash stopped beside the child. "Thanks for helping Jedidiah drive today, Matthew. Do you think the two of you can find Naomi Walker's house?"

"I'll make sure he doesn't get lost." The boy's solemn tone showed he was taking his responsibility seriously, but he grinned at his stepfather. Jedidiah snatched up the boy's hat and ruffled his hair affectionately.

Two months ago, Ash had stood beside Jedediah as he wed Mary Kate. Today, Jedidiah would return the favor by being one of Ash's groomsmen along with his brothers.

A week after their wedding, Mary Kate and Jedidiah had arrived back in New Covenant with her quiet son. The community rallied to make the somber child feel welcome by holding a picnic at the school to introduce him to the other children. In the few short weeks that he had been with his mother and his new family, Matthew was coming out of his shell. Jedediah opened the buggy door, and the boy scrambled onto the front seat.

"Ready for this?" Jedidiah asked Ash.

Ash grinned and clapped his neighbor on the shoulder. "I've never been more ready for anything in my life. Drive fast."

"Are you sure I look okay?" Mari cast imploring glances at her *newehockers*—her side-sitters, the three women who would be her attendants during the ceremony and afterward at the wedding feast. Pamela, Esther and Mary Kate were all dressed as Mari was in identical pale blue dresses with white capes and aprons. As the bride, only Mari wore a black *kapp*. She would trade it for a white one later in the day.

"You look lovely," Mary Kate said. "Like a woman who is madly in love."

Mari closed her eyes. "I don't know how it is possible to love someone so much. *Gott* has blessed me beyond all measure."

"He has blessed both of us," Mary Kate said. "I came to Maine desperate to marry and get my son back. Instead of the loveless union I expected with Asher, I found Jedidiah, a kind and generous man who takes my breath away and two lovely little girls who asked me yesterday if they could call me Mother. I have my son and a new family I adore. I never imagined my life could be so wonderful."

Mari clasped Mary Kate's hands between her own. "I don't think I could have been truly happy knowing I took Ash away from you, but now I don't have to worry. I'll never forget the sacrifice you were willing to make for our love."

"I couldn't keep the two of you apart after I learned how Ash felt about you. Jedidiah was my reward for making the right decision. At least that's what he likes to tell me," she said with a chuckle as a blush stained her cheeks.

Naomi opened the door to her bedroom where the women were waiting. "Mari, your friends from Arthur have arrived."

"Wunderbar. Have them come in." She had written to the women she'd worked with in the fabric shop back home detailing her adventures and included an invitation to the wedding. Her three friends came in grinning from ear to ear.

"Mari, we're so happy for you." They each hugged her in turn. One handed her a package. "This came in the mail before we left."

"For me?" Mari looked at the return address. It had been mailed from the bus depot in Caribou, Maine. "I wonder what it could be."

She tore open the brown paper wrapping. Inside a cardboard box was a black bag. "My purse!"

She held it up. Until this moment she hadn't recalled anything leading up to her accident. "I remember now. I forgot my purse on the bus. I ran after the bus to try and stop it. That's why I dashed into the road. The man who hit me wasn't at fault. I was."

Inside was a note saying the purse had been turned into lost and found, and was being mailed to the owner's address found on her checkbook.

Mari looked up at Naomi. "We must let the State Police know."

"We will. After the wedding. Ash is here."

Mari's heart gave a happy leap. "It's really happening, isn't it? I'm getting married."

Naomi grinned. She wore a dark green Amish dress and a white *kapp*. "Yes, and I am so grateful to be a part of your special day."

After weeks of soul-searching, Naomi chose to return to the Amish faith and was accepted into the New Covenant congregation. Her shunning was now a thing of the past and would never be mentioned again.

Mari stepped into her grandmother's embrace. "I can't believe how blessed I am to have found you."

"I love you. All I want is for you to be happy," Naomi whispered. "Ash does make you happy, doesn't he?"

"He does." Mari couldn't stop smiling. Ash was everything she could ever want. Just the thought of being his wife sent shivers of excitement down her spine.

"It's time to go," Pamela said.

Mari stepped back and clasped her hands together. "I guess I'm ready."

The others filed out of the room. Mari took a deep breath and followed.

Ash was standing by the front door. His eyes

lit up at the sight of her. The attendants paired up and walked into the living room.

A grin curved Ash's lips. "You haven't forgotten that we are getting married today, have you?"

Her last bit of nervousness fled at the love shining in his eyes. "I knew there was something I was supposed to be doing this morning."

He held out his hand. She took it, and he squeezed her fingers. "This *is* the day *which* the Lord hath made."

"We will rejoice and be glad in it," she finished the verse, knowing it was impossible to be any happier.

Hand in hand they walked in to join the bishop where they declared their love in front of God and the whole church, to begin their new life together just as God had planned.

* * * * *

If you enjoyed this story, look for these other North Country Amish books by Patricia Davids:

An Amish Wife for Christmas
Shelter from the Storm
The Amish Teacher's Dilemma
A Haven for Christmas
Someone to Trust
An Amish Mother for His Twins

Dear Reader,

I'm writing this in my little farmhouse in Kansas. The view from my windows is of wide, open spaces, blue sky and lilac bushes loaded with blooms. The endless wheat fields are carpets of emerald green. It's spring.

My CH kitten Weeble is patiently waiting for me to finish writing today so we can play. My dog Sugar is at my feet waiting for the same thing. It's nice to be wanted.

Our lives are a fabric made of memories. I tried to imagine what a rip in that fabric would do to a young woman named Mari. It became an interesting and fascinating journey for me as I crafted this story. I hope you enjoyed it.

The Fisher family has been a joy to write about and I'm not done with New Covenant, Maine. I have Moses to marry off. Danny, the teacher, needs to find his soul mate. Who knows who else will pop up from my imagination? I hope you'll follow along when they do.

Blessings,
Patricia Davids

Get 4 FREE REWARDS!

We'll send you 2 FREE Books plus 2 FREE Mystery Gifts.

FREE
Value Over
$20

Both the **Love Inspired®** and **Love Inspired®** Suspense series feature compelling novels filled with inspirational romance, faith, forgiveness, and hope.

Get 4 FREE REWARDS!

We'll send you 2 FREE Books plus 2 FREE Mystery Gifts.

FREE Value Over **$20**

Both the **Harlequin® Special Edition** and **Harlequin® Heartwarming™** series feature compelling novels filled with stories of love and strength where the bonds of friendship, family and community unite.

YES! Please send me 2 FREE novels from the Harlequin Special Edition or Harlequin Heartwarming series and my 2 FREE gifts (gifts are worth about $10 retail). After receiving them, if I don't wish to receive any more books, I can return the shipping statement marked "cancel." If I don't cancel, I will receive 6 brand-new Harlequin Special Edition books every month and be billed just $4.99 each in the U.S or $5.74 each in Canada, a savings of at least 17% off the cover price or 4 brand-new Harlequin Heartwarming Larger-Print books every month and be billed just $5.74 each in the U.S. or $6.24 each in Canada, a savings of at least 21% off the cover price. It's quite a bargain! Shipping and handling is just 50¢ per book in the U.S. and $1.25 per book in Canada.* I understand that accepting the 2 free books and gifts places me under no obligation to buy anything. I can always return a shipment and cancel at any time. The free books and gifts are mine to keep no matter what I decide.

Choose one: ☐ **Harlequin Special Edition** ☐ **Harlequin Heartwarming**
(235/335 HDN GNMP) **Larger-Print**
(161/361 HDN GNPZ)

Name (please print)

Address _____ Apt. #

City _____ State/Province _____ Zip/Postal Code

Email: Please check this box ☐ if you would like to receive newsletters and promotional emails from Harlequin Enterprises ULC and its affiliates. You can unsubscribe anytime.

Mail to the **Harlequin Reader Service:**
IN U.S.A.: P.O. Box 1341, Buffalo, NY 14240-8531
IN CANADA: P.O. Box 603, Fort Erie, Ontario L2A 5X3

Want to try 2 free books from another series? Call 1-800-873-8635 or visit www.ReaderService.com.

*Terms and prices subject to change without notice. Prices do not include sales taxes, which will be charged (if applicable) based on your state or country of residence. Canadian residents will be charged applicable taxes. Offer not valid in Quebec. This offer is limited to one order per household. Books received may not be as shown. Not valid for current subscribers to the Harlequin Special Edition or Harlequin Heartwarming series. All orders subject to approval. Credit or debit balances in a customer's account(s) may be offset by any other outstanding balance owed by or to the customer. Please allow 4 to 6 weeks for delivery. Offer available while quantities last.

Your Privacy—Your information is being collected by Harlequin Enterprises ULC, operating as Harlequin Reader Service. For a complete summary of the information we collect, how we use this information and to whom it is disclosed, please visit our privacy notice located at corporate.harlequin.com/privacy-notice. From time to time we may also exchange your personal information with reputable third parties. If you wish to opt out of this sharing of your personal information, please visit readerservice.com/consumerchoice or call 1-800-873-8635. **Notice to California Residents**—Under California law, you have specific rights to control and access your data. For more information on these rights and how to exercise them, visit corporate.harlequin.com/california-privacy.

HSEHW22

COUNTRY LEGACY COLLECTION

19 FREE BOOKS IN ALL!

EMMETT
Diana Palmer

COURTED BY THE COWBOY

THE RANCHER AND THE BABY
Marie Ferrarella

Cowboys, adventure and romance await you in this new collection! Enjoy superb reading all year long with books by bestselling authors like Diana Palmer, Sasha Summers and Marie Ferrarella!

COMING NEXT MONTH FROM
Love Inspired

THE AMISH TWINS NEXT DOOR
Indiana Amish Brides • by Vannetta Chapman

Amish single mom Deborah Mast is determined to raise her seven-year-old twin sons *her* way. But when neighbor Nicholas Stoltzfus takes on the rambunctious boys as apprentices on his farm, she'll learn the value of his help with more than just the children—including how to reopen her heart.

SECRETS IN AN AMISH GARDEN
Amish Seasons • by Lenora Worth

When garden nursery owner Rebecca Eicher hires a new employee, she can't help but notice that Jebediah Martin looks similar to her late fiancé. But when her brother plays matchmaker, Jeb's secret is on the brink of being revealed. Will the truth bring them together or break them apart forever?

EARNING HER TRUST
K-9 Companions • by Brenda Minton

With the help of her service dog, Zeb, Emery Guthrie is finally living a life free from her childhood trauma. Then her high school bully, Beau Wilde, returns to town to care for his best friend's orphaned daughters. Has she healed enough to truly forgive him and let him into her life?

THEIR ALASKAN PAST
Home to Owl Creek • by Belle Calhoune

Opening a dog rescue in Owl Creek, Alaska, is a dream come true for veterinarian Maya Roberts, but the only person she can get to help her run it is her ex-boyfriend Ace Reynolds. When a financial situation forces Ace to accept the position, Maya can't run from her feelings...or the secret of why she ended things.

A NEED TO PROTECT
Widow's Peak Creek • by Susanne Dietze

Dairy shepherdess Clementine Simon's only concern is the safety of her orphaned niece and nephew and *not* the return of her former love Liam Murphy. But could the adventuring globe-trotter be just what she needs to overcome her fears and take another chance on love?

A PROMISE FOR HIS DAUGHTER
by Danielle Thorne

After arriving in Kudzu Creek, contractor and historical preservationist Bradley Ainsworth discovers the two-year-old daughter he never knew about living there with her foster mom, Claire Woodbury. But as they work together updating the house Claire owns, he might find the family he didn't know he was missing...

LICNM0322